From Friendship To Marriage

And Beyond

By

Dr. John L. Jacobs, III

Table of Contents

DEDICATION

I dedicate this book to my four children as you navigate your way through relationships. I pray that my experiences through this book will save you from headache, heartache, and unnecessary relationship issues. As your Dad, it is my desire that you meet that special person with whom you can happily spend the rest of your lives with.

INTRODUCTION

Love is a journey, and a journey begins with a single step. When you talk about relationships, there is perhaps no more profound and heartwarming journey than the one that takes you from friendship to marriage. It is a journey filled with laughter, tears, shared dreams, and the indomitable strength of two hearts uniting to create a life together. "From Friendship to Marriage and Beyond" is a story of love, companionship, and the enduring power of friendship as the foundation for a lifelong relationship.

Friendship, the foundation of this transformation, is a unique bond. It's a connection that goes beyond mere acquaintance, where two individuals find resonance and share their joys and sorrows. From the moment two people meet, sparks may fly, or a deep and lasting connection may form, but the path to a lifelong commitment is paved with intention and a deepening understanding of one another.

This book uncovers the beautiful evolution of a relationship, from the initial sparks of friendship to the sacred vows of marriage, and further explores the uncharted territories of life beyond the wedding day. It's a journey where friendship is not lost but instead enhanced by the complexities and joys of marriage. You'll explore challenges and triumphs as relationships navigate through this ever-evolving journey of love.

Friendship provides a strong foundation upon which couples can build their lives together. It's a relationship that fosters understanding, compassion, and unwavering support for one another. As this friendship deepens, the transition to a romantic relationship becomes a natural progression, leading to the ultimate commitment of marriage.

This book will take you on a journey that touches upon the art of communication, the power of compromise, and the beauty of shared dreams. It will also address the challenges couples encounter, such as disagreements, external pressures, and personal growth. But it will underscore the resilience of love that can weather all storms.

Furthermore, you will explore the adventures that unfold beyond marriage, parenthood, career aspirations, and shared aspirations for the future. The journey doesn't stop with a wedding; instead, it continues to evolve and transform, presenting new opportunities for growth and shared experiences.

In "From Friendship to Marriage and Beyond," you will explore the profound and beautiful transformation of how two people can come together as friends and emerge as lifelong 'companions.' It is a journey of love, personal growth, and a testament to the enduring power of friendship as the cornerstone of a fulfilling and lasting marriage. Let's embark on this emotional, inspiring, and trans formative journey into the heart of relationships and the remarkable story of love that goes from friendship to marriage and beyond.

CHAPTER 1

TRUE FRIENDS ARE HARD TO FIND

How many TRUE friends do you have? How many can you depend on? TRUE Friends are hard to come by. What most people call friends are more than likely acquaintances or associates.

A true friend can be hard to find. Friends are those whom you can talk to in times of need and trust that rumors will not spread because you tell someone something personal about yourself.

A friend is one who will help you when you can't help yourself and tell you the truth regardless of whether you like it or not. A true friend respects you to the point that they want the best for you not because of how you can benefit them but because of who you are, what you stand for, and what you mean to them.

You can't buy true friendship; it has to be earned. A friend is normally not a biological family member but feels closer than family through their genuine love, respect, and sacrifice. A true friend is someone who goes beyond the superficial and shares a deep connection with you. They offer unwavering support, trust, and loyalty.

True friends are those who stand by you through both good times and bad, offering a sense of companionship that is irreplaceable. Becoming a friend involves a gradual process of building a connection, trust, and mutual understanding. Most friendships start with a simple interaction, like a conversation or shared activity.

This can happen in various settings, such as school, work, social events, church, online communities, etc. Shared interests, hobbies, or values can be a strong foundation for friendship. When you discover common ground with someone, it becomes easier to bond and relate to each other.

In order to develop a friendship, consistent and meaningful communication is essential. This can involve regular conversations, both in person and virtually, through calls, messages, or social media. Trust is a fundamental aspect of friendship. As you get to know someone, you learn to trust them, and they learn to trust you. Being reliable and keeping promises is vital in building this trust.

True friendships often involve a degree of vulnerability. Sharing your thoughts, feelings, and experiences with a friend can deepen the connection. Being open and non-judgmental creates a safe space for both individuals to express themselves. True friends should be there for each other in times of need. Offering emotional support and empathy when facing challenges or celebrating successes.

Shared experiences, both positive and negative, help strengthen the bond between individuals. These experiences can include travel, adventures, celebrations, or even going through difficult times together. Building a genuine friendship takes time. Consistency in your interactions and efforts to maintain the relationship is essential for it to grow and flourish. Respecting each other's boundaries and personal space is vital in any friendship.

It's important to understand and acknowledge the comfort levels of your friends and not push them into situations they are not ready for. A true friend always wants the best for you and will not coerce you to do anything against the law or your moral standards. A true friend has your best interest at heart.

Conflicts and misunderstandings can arise in any relationship. Being able to forgive and work through these issues is a sign of a strong and lasting friendship. Open and honest communication is key to resolving conflicts. Friendship should be a two-way street. Both individuals should contribute to the relationship, offering support, kindness, and care to for each other.

Having fun together and sharing moments of laughter can make a friendship more enjoyable. A sense of humor and shared laughter can strengthen the emotional bond. True friends hold a special place in your life. They are confidants, companions, and sources of emotional support. A friend is someone you can turn to when you need advice, encouragement, or simply a listening ear.

They are there to celebrate your successes and provide comfort during your failures. Having friends offers a wide range of benefits, both for your mental and emotional well-being. They provide a support system to help you navigate life's challenges and share your joys and sorrows. They can offer comfort, a listening ear, and empathy during difficult times.

Loneliness can have detrimental effects on mental and physical health; however, having friends can help combat loneliness by providing companionship and a sense of belonging. Spending time with friends can help reduce stress. Conversations, laughter, and enjoyable activities release endorphins and lower stress hormones.

Positive social interactions with friends can boost your mood and contribute to greater overall happiness as well as sharing laughter, and fun experiences can have a significant impact on your well-being. Friends can boost your self-esteem by offering positive reinforcement, compliments, and a sense of belonging.

They can remind you of your strengths and accomplishments. Having friends is associated with better mental health outcomes and provides emotional support, which can be especially valuable in times of anxiety, depression, or stress. Having friends can help you develop better coping mechanisms when facing challenges.

They offer different perspectives and insights that can assist you in finding solutions to problems. It has been found that individuals with strong social connections tend to live longer, healthier lives. Friends can encourage healthier habits and provide a safety net during times of illness or need. Sometimes, they come from various backgrounds and have different life experiences.

This diversity can expose you to new ideas, cultures, and viewpoints, broadening your horizons and promoting personal growth. Interacting with friends helps you develop and refine social skills, such as communication, empathy, and conflict resolution, which can be valuable in both personal and professional relationships.

True Friends challenge you to step out of your comfort zone, try new things, and achieve personal goals. They can provide motivation and support for self-improvement. They can also introduce you to valuable networking opportunities, assist you in meeting new people, share career opportunities, or accompany you to social events.

Friends can be a source of fun and enjoyment in your life, and they can make everyday activities more entertaining by sharing memorable experiences with you. Friends can provide a sense of belonging, acceptance, and being part of a social group can be calming and affirming. Friendships may come in various forms, and people play different roles in your life.

Childhood friends (these are friends you've known since your early years, often from school or your neighborhood) hold a special place in your heart, and they share memories and experiences from your formative years. Work friends are those you interact with primarily in a professional setting.

While the relationship may start at work, it can evolve into a genuine friendship based on shared interests and support. College friends are friends you meet while pursing higher education; they share academic interests and may become lifelong friends. With the emergence of the internet and social media, many people form friendships with individuals they may have never met in person.

These online friends can be from all over the world and share common interests or experiences. These friends are united by a shared passion or interest, such as sports, art, music, video games, or a particular hobby that centers around a common pursuit. Community or neighborhood friends are individuals who live in or around your community or neighborhood.

You may interact with them in casual settings, like block parties or mixers, and rely on them for local support. Travel friends are people you meet while exploring the world. One may bond over the shared experience of discovering new places, cultures, and foods.

Supportive friends are friends who provide a strong support system during challenging times.

One can count on them when you need help, whether it's emotional, financial, physical, or practical. Not all people you associate with are friends; some may be acquaintances or associates. You have a friendly but limited relationship with these people, often based on shared activities or common friends. You share light, enjoyable interactions with these friends but not necessarily deep emotional connections.

You might hang out occasionally or have fun at social events. Long-distance friends are individuals who live far away but maintain a meaningful connection through communication, visits, and shared experiences whenever possible. A best friend is often considered a soulmate, someone who knows you deeply and you share an unbreakable bond.

They are your confidant and the person you turn to for most things. Some friendships endure over the years and become lifelong connections. These friends have seen you evolve through various life stages and remain a constant presence in your life. Unfortunately, not all friendships are deep and lasting.

Fair-weather friends are there when times are good but may disappear during challenging periods. If you have shared faith or spiritual beliefs, friends from your religious or spiritual community can provide a unique source of support and camaraderie. Adventurous friends share your love for adrenaline-pumping activities, whether it's extreme sports, hiking, skydiving, or other daring experiences.

Each type of friendship serves a different purpose in your life, and it's important to recognize and appreciate the diverse roles that friends play. Some friends may be more transient, while others become lifelong companions. The key is to nurture and cherish the friendships that bring positive interactions and meaning to your life.

Building a foundation on friendship before entering a romantic relationship can be invaluable. A strong friendship forms the basis of trust and understanding, enhancing the quality and longevity of a romantic relationship.

CHAPTER 2

WAIT ON GOD

In the vast symphony of life, where your desires and dreams play the melodies of your hearts, there is a quiet, soulful refrain that speaks of waiting. Waiting on God is an art that requires patience, trust, and an unwavering belief in divine timing. When it comes to the profound quest for love, waiting on God takes on a unique significance rooted in faith, wisdom, and the profound understanding that God's plan is far greater than your own.

Prayer is a powerful tool in the journey of seeking a life partner. When you pray, you open communication with God, allowing Him to guide your thoughts, feelings, and decisions. Prayer isn't just about asking for what you want; it's about aligning your desires with God's will. As you seek a special person for a relationship and marriage, you must pray for clarity, wisdom, and discernment.

You should ask God to reveal His plan and His timing in this area of your life. You should also pray for the person you hope to meet or already know, asking God to work in their lives. This brings you closer to God and strengthens your connection with the person you're interested in. Prayer is not a one-way conversation. It is also about listening to God's voice. In your haste to find a partner, you often neglect the importance of stillness and listening. God speaks to you in various ways – through His word, the counsel of wise individuals, and the inner promptings of your heart. Taking the time to listen to God's voice is crucial.

It can help you discern whether the person you are interested in aligns with God's plan for your life. Sometimes, God may gently steer you away from someone who seems perfect on the surface but doesn't share your values and life goals. Divine timing is the essence of waiting on God and recognizing that divine timing transcends your human schedules and desires.

In your pursuit of love, it's natural to want it now and to reach out to grasp what your heart longs for. Yet, God's timing is perfect and precise, aligning with the intricate tapestry of your life in ways you may not fully comprehend. When you wait on God, you acknowledge that a divine plan is unfolding, one that may require you to be patient.

This patience is not passive; it is a proactive trust in the unfolding of God's design. It means surrendering your desire for immediate gratification and allowing God to orchestrate the right moments and encounters. Praying, listening, and waiting on God is not merely about enduring the passage of time; it's about actively seeking His guidance and listening for His voice.

Prayer becomes a powerful companion on this journey. Through prayer, you lay your hopes, fears, and desires before God, inviting His wisdom and discernment into your hearts. In the quiet moments of prayer, you create a sacred space where you can listen to God's whispers. His guidance may come in the form of intuition, a still, small voice, or a profound sense of peace. By listening attentively, you align your desires with His divine plan.

Impatience can lead you to accept counterfeits in your pursuit of love. you may encounter relationships that seem promising, individuals who tick many of your boxes, and situations that offer the illusion of love. Yet, in your eagerness to find love, you can easily mistake these counterfeits for the real thing.

Waiting on God requires the discernment to distinguish between what is genuine and what is not. It means being willing to step back, even when your emotions urge you to move forward. It means being discerning and patient, trusting that God will reveal His best when the time is right. In the journey of waiting on God, it's essential to acknowledge that you may make mistakes.

You might misinterpret His guidance or act on your own impulses. But here is where the beauty of divine love shines—God's grace is boundless. When you err, when you stray from His path, God is not a stern judge waiting to condemn us. Instead, He is a loving Father, ready to embrace His wayward children when they return. Transparency is the key.

You must be honest with God and with yourselves about your missteps, your moments of confusion, and your attempts to forge ahead without His guidance. In these moments of honesty and humility, you grow, your faith deepens, and you become more attuned to God's voice. You learn to trust His plan even when it seems mysterious, knowing that He is weaving a beautiful story of love in the fabric of your life.

In the pursuit of love, impatience can be a formidable adversary. you may encounter individuals who seem close to what you desire in a partner, but they are not ready or able to fulfill the requirements of a lasting relationship. In your impatience, you might attempt to mold them into your ideal partner, only to find yourselves in a miserable mismatch.

This is a common pitfall listening to your own voice or the voices of others instead of waiting on God's perfect timing and His choice for us. The journey to finding a mate can be long and winding, but it's vital to remain diligent in waiting on God. His timing is impeccable, and His choice is tailor-made for us.

Remember, while impatience may lead to pitfalls, patience can open the door to a love that is worth the wait—a love that is built on a strong foundation, mutual understanding, and the beautiful unfolding of God's plan. When you wait on God, you trust that He will lead you to a love that surpasses your wildest dreams, a love that is rooted in His divine wisdom and boundless grace.

In the silence of your soul, where the deepest desires reside, you often strain to hear the voice of God. you long for His guidance, especially when it comes to matters of the heart. Yet, amidst the stillness, a cacophony of voices can arise, each vying for your attention. In your quest to discern God's will, you can sometimes conjure a voice that sounds like His, a voice that aligns with your hopes and desires.

It's a voice that tells you what you want to hear, soothing your anxieties and insecurities. But it's not always God's voice. With its practicality and logic, the voice of reason can make a convincing argument for certain choices. Fear, with its crippling grip, can whisper tales of caution, urging you to stay within your comfort zones.

Need and desire, driven by the thirst for companionship, can clamor loudly, drowning out the gentle whisper of God's guidance. Yet, amidst this symphony of voices, you must learn to distinguish the divine melody. When God speaks, manifestations occur. His words are not mere echoes in the chambers of your heart; they are promises that come to life as His plans unfold with divine precision.

In these moments, when you align your heart with His word, the path becomes clear. The confusion dissipates, and the doubts recede like morning mist before the sun. When you hear His voice, you sense a profound peace, an inner knowing that transcends the doubts and fears that often cloud your judgment.

But let's be honest, sometimes you miss the mark. In your eagerness to find love and make choices that promise immediate fulfillment, you mistake God's voice for another. you step onto a path that seems well-lit but is a detour. you choose partners who may not be the ones God had intended for us.

In these moments of misalignment, you must not despair. God is not a harsh judge waiting to condemn you for your errors. Instead, He is a loving Father, ready to embrace His wayward children when they return. To receive His grace, you must be honest with Him and yourselves. you must acknowledge your mistakes, your moments of misguided judgment, and your attempts to forge ahead without His guidance.

God understands your humanity and your capacity for confusion. He knows that your heart often leads you astray. But He also knows that within you lies the potential for growth, wisdom, and discernment.

When you admit your errors and seek His guidance anew, He lovingly steers you back onto the path of His divine will.

The whispers within are not always easy to discern, but they are worth the effort. As you embark on this journey to find a mate, remember to listen attentively, wait patiently, and trust in the guidance that transcends the noise of the world. For within those whispers lies the wisdom of God, guiding you toward a love that is not of this world but is rooted in the divine.

In the grand tapestry of life, where your stories are woven with threads of joy, sorrow, and longing, there are moments when you, with the best of intentions, miss the mark. This chapter explores one such facet of your journey—those times when you yearn for love so ardently that you stumble in your pursuit of it.

You often stand at the crossroads of desire and patience in pursuing love. you feel the urgency of your heart's longing, a deep yearning for companionship, and the warmth of love's embrace. Yet, in your haste to find what your soul craves, you can inadvertently take missteps, like a traveler on an unfamiliar path. Sometimes, the voices within you can be like a tumultuous sea, tossing you to and fro.

You mistake God's voice for another, perhaps the voice of your desires, fears, or the well-meaning counsel of friends and family. In your fervor to fill the void, you might imagine God's approval of your decisions, even when the divine path remains veiled. In these moments of misalignment, you must practice humility and introspection.

For God, Who is ever-loving and understanding, does not condemn you for your well-intentioned errors. Instead, He waits patiently, like a wise parent, for you to recognize your mistakes. He offers you the grace to return to the path He has chosen for us. When you miss Him, you must summon the courage to admit it. you must be transparent with God and with yourselves.

Such honesty is the key that unlocks the door to His boundless grace. God's love is unconditional, and His forgiveness knows no bounds. But you must be willing to acknowledge your errors, for only then can you fully embrace the lessons He has prepared for us. In the realm of relationships, particularly in the quest for a life mate, impatience can be a formidable adversary. you may encounter individuals who seem promising, close to the ideal you envision in a partner. Yet, they may not be ready or able to fulfill the requirements of a lasting and meaningful connection. Impatience can lead you to mold them into your ideal, hoping that time and effort will bridge the gaps.

However, the truth is that love cannot be rushed. It cannot be forced or manufactured. Love flourishes when it unfolds naturally when two souls come together in their own time and in their own unique way. When you attempt to expedite the process, you often find yourselves in a relationship that is far from the harmonious union you envisioned.

You may realize that you have tried to fit a square peg into a round hole, and the result is discomfort and heartache. This serves as a reminder, a gentle tug at the sleeves of your hearts, to exercise patience and wisdom in the pursuit of love. It urges you to wait on

God's timing, to listen intently for His voice, and to trust in His plan, even when your desires pull you in different directions.

The journey to finding a life partner is not a sprint but a marathon, a winding path filled with lessons and discoveries. As you continue on this journey together, remember that every misstep is an opportunity to learn and grow. God's guidance is ever-present, waiting for you to align your heart with His divine will, and in doing so, you find not just love but a love that is blessed by His grace.

In the grand tapestry of life, where your stories are woven with threads of joy, sorrow, and longing, there are moments when you, with the best of intentions, miss the mark. This chapter explores one such facet of your journey—those times when you yearn for love so ardently that you stumble in your pursuit of it.

In the pursuit of love, you often stand at the crossroads of desire and patience. you feel the urgency of your heart's longing, a deep yearning for companionship, and the warmth of love's embrace. Yet, in your haste to find what your soul craves, you can inadvertently take missteps, like a traveler on an unfamiliar path.

Impatience is a powerful force that often drives you to act before you fully understand the consequences of your choices. In the realm of love, impatience can manifest as a burning desire to find "the one" quickly. A sense of urgency can compel you to rush into relationships or make hasty judgments about potential partners.

The impatient heart sees time as an enemy, constantly ticking away, and it believes that finding love must happen sooner rather than later. It fears that opportunities will slip through its fingers, leaving it alone and unfulfilled. Impatience whispers in your ears, "Why wait? Seize the moment. Take a chance."

Impatience in the pursuit of love can lead you down treacherous paths and often manifests in several common pitfalls. One of the most significant pitfalls of impatience is settling for less, settling for a relationship that does not truly align with your values, desires, and long-term goals. When you rush into a relationship out of impatience, you may compromise on important aspects, hoping that time will bridge the gaps.

In doing so, you may find yourselves in a partnership that falls short of your expectations, causing frustration and heartache. Impatience can blind you to red flags and warning signs in a potential partner. you might overlook character flaws or compatibility issues, believing that these can be worked out later.

This can lead to entering a relationship fraught with challenges and unmet expectations.

Impatience can drive you to commit to a relationship prematurely. Instead of allowing love to evolve naturally and grow at its own pace, you might push for exclusivity or even marriage before truly getting to know your partner.

This can put unnecessary pressure on the relationship and hinder its development. Impatience can also strain existing relationships. When you are eagerly searching for love, you might become restless or dissatisfied with your current partner. This can lead to conflict and unhappiness within the relationship, even if it was initially strong.

In a world that often urges you to embrace instant gratification and seize opportunities without hesitation, the concept of waiting can seem counterintuitive, even frustrating. Yet, there is a profound and transformative power in the act of waiting, particularly when pursuing love.

Waiting is not merely the absence of action; it is a deliberate choice, a conscious decision to exercise patience and trust in a process that unfolds at its own pace.

In the realm of love, waiting is a virtue that can shape the course of your relationships, leading you to deeper connections, meaningful partnerships, and a love that endures. Waiting allows you the time and space to clarify your values, desires, and goals in a relationship. It encourages self-discovery, enabling you to understand what you truly need in a partner and what you can offer in return.

Waiting also offers the opportunity for discernment. It allows you to evaluate potential partners with a discerning eye, taking the time to get to know them on a deeper level. It involves asking important questions and assessing compatibility, values, and long-term vision. Patience enables you to build strong foundations for relationships.

It allows love to develop organically, allowing both partners to grow together and create a solid bond based on trust, understanding, and shared experiences. For those who believe in a higher power, waiting can be an act of faith and trust in divine timing. It acknowledges that there is a greater plan at work, one that may unfold in unexpected and beautiful ways.

Taking care of oneself physically, emotionally, and spiritually while patiently awaiting the right partner. Self-care ensures that you are in the best possible state to give and receive love. Practicing patience and embracing the idea that love will come in its own time, not necessarily on your schedule. Turning to trusted friends, mentors, or spiritual advisors for guidance and wisdom during the waiting period. Engaging in hobbies, interests, and passions that bring joy and fulfillment independently of a romantic relationship.

Remaining open to new connections and experiences while understanding that not every encounter must lead to a lifelong partnership. The act of waiting on God is rooted in a profound trust in His wisdom, love, and timing. It is a testament to your faith that His plan is greater than your own. As you navigate the complex and beautiful journey of finding a mate, you must remember that your understanding is limited, but His is boundless.

CHAPTER 3

EXPRESSING EXPECTATIONS

When considering a long-term friendship or relationship, expressing your expectations is important. Open and honest communication is the cornerstone of any healthy relationship, and it is imperative when you are contemplating embarking on a journey with someone special.

Expressing expectations is vital to fostering understanding, trust, and harmony between two people.

Open and honest communication about what each person hopes to achieve, experience, and contribute can set the foundation for a healthy and fulfilling partnership. It also helps clarify the roles and responsibilities of each person. Verbalizing your expectations outlines who is responsible for what, which is essential for ensuring that both individuals are on the same page and that there are no unspoken assumptions or misunderstandings.

It allows both parties to better understand each other's desires, needs, and goals. This mutual understanding can lead to more empathetic and supportive interactions. Unexpressed or unmet expectations can lead to conflicts. By openly communicating your expectations, you reduce the likelihood of misunderstandings and disagreements.

This proactive approach can prevent unnecessary tension in the relationship. Trust is built on the belief that two people will meet their expectations and commitments. When both individuals communicate their expectations and work towards fulfilling them, it enhances trust and reliability.

Expressing expectations requires vulnerability and emotional openness. It provides an opportunity for both individuals to connect on a deeper emotional level as they share their hopes, fears, and desires with each other. Both individuals should have aligned goals and visions for the future.

Expressing expectations allows both people to assess whether their individual goals are compatible and whether they can work together towards shared milestones. When issues or conflicts arise, clear communication of expectations provides a foundation for effective problem-solving. When working through challenges, mutually understood expectations can be referred to.

Our expectations can change over time as individuals and circumstances evolve. Openly discussing and adjusting expectations as needed promotes adaptability and personal growth. Expressing expectations about the type of quality time and activities each person values can help ensure that both individuals feel satisfied and cherished.

Communicating expectations is a way of showing respect for each other's feelings and desires. It demonstrates that you value each other's perspective and are willing to work together to meet both individuals' needs. Practicing active listening, empathy, and clear communication is essential to effectively expressing expectations.

Both individuals should feel comfortable sharing their expectations and actively listening to each other's desires and concerns. Constructive and respectful dialogue is key to building a strong foundation of shared understanding and trust. A fulfilling and enduring understanding can be created by openly expressing expectations and working together to meet them.

The significance of expressing expectations, particularly in the context of considering a long-term commitment, cannot be overstated. It plays a crucial role in shaping the dynamics and success of the friendship or relationship. Expressing expectations helps define the roles and responsibilities of each person.

When both individuals are aware of what is expected of them, it reduces confusion and prevents conflicts stemming from unmet expectations. This clarity ensures that both individuals are on the same page and working towards common goals. However, this won't work if either person is unwilling to accept the role discussed for each other.

Each must agree and accept with total commitment to their individual roles. Wavering on your commitment can cause mistrust, heartache, and confusion. Misunderstandings are a common source of tension. By openly discussing and expressing expectations, individuals can minimize misunderstandings and misinterpretations.

This proactive communication style reduces the likelihood of arguments and disagreements arising due to assumptions or unspoken desires. Trust is a fundamental building block. Trust is strengthened when two people express their expectations and actively work towards meeting them.

Trust is not just about fidelity; it also encompasses trust in each other's commitment and confidence that responsibilities will be fulfilled. Trust forms the foundation for a lasting, secure bond.

Conflict is inevitable, but how conflicts are handled can make a significant difference. When expectations are openly communicated, conflicts can be addressed more effectively. Different viewpoints among individuals can be discussed to find compromises and solutions that satisfy them both. Expressing expectations requires vulnerability and emotional honesty. This vulnerability fosters emotional intimacy, allowing individuals to connect more deeply. When you share your expectations, you are revealing your desires, fears, and hopes, which can lead to a more profound emotional connection.

As individuals evolve over time, so do expectations. Continuously expressing and revisiting expectations can adapt to changing circumstances and personal growth. This adaptability is essential for long-term success and resilience. The act of expressing expectations involves effective communication.

It encourages individuals to practice active listening, empathy, and understanding. These communication skills are valuable in friendships or relationships and other life aspects. While admitting fault may not be easy it fosters a pathway to embrace personal growth. Both components are critical aspects of development.

These actions demonstrate maturity, self-awareness, and a commitment to building stronger, more fulfilling connections with others. Admitting when you're wrong or have made a mistake shows humility. It acknowledges that nobody is perfect and everyone is capable of errors. This humility can be endearing and create a more empathetic and understanding atmosphere.

Acknowledging your mistakes and taking responsibility for them helps build trust with others. When people know that you are honest about your shortcomings, they are more likely to trust you in other aspects of life. Taking ownership of your actions and their consequences fosters accountability.

This accountability can lead to positive changes in behavior because you are actively recognizing and addressing areas where improvement is needed. Admitting fault often opens the door to productive conversations. It allows both parties to discuss the issue, understand each other's perspectives, and work together to find solutions or compromises.

Unresolved conflicts or unacknowledged mistakes can lead to resentment and emotional distance. Admitting fault and addressing issues promptly can prevent the buildup of negative emotions and hurt feelings. When you admit your mistakes, it becomes easier for others to forgive us. In many cases, genuine remorse and a willingness to make amends can lead to forgiveness and reconciliation.

Acknowledging your faults and mistakes is the first step toward personal growth. It allows you to identify areas where you can improve, develop new skills, and become a better version of yourself. Individuals who actively seek personal growth often contribute positively to their friendships or relationships.

As you grow and evolve, you can bring new perspectives, improved communication skills, and a deeper understanding of yourself and others. Embracing growth means you are more adaptable and resilient in the face of challenges. You become better equipped to handle change and navigate difficult situations, which can benefit both your personal and professional life.

As you make progress in personal growth, your self-esteem and self-confidence tend to improve. You gain a sense of accomplishment and self-worth from your journey of self-improvement. Your commitment to growth can inspire those around you. When others see you actively working on your flaws and striving to become a better person, they may be motivated to do the same.

Personal growth is a lifelong journey. It encourages continuous learning and self-discovery, which can be fulfilling and enriching throughout your life. Open communication is the key to any healthy and successful relationship, and its significance cannot be overstated.

Whether in a romantic relationship, a friendship, a family relationship, or a professional setting, open communication plays a pivotal role in fostering understanding, trust, and positive outcomes. Open communication allows individuals to express their thoughts, feelings, and perspectives openly and honestly.

It provides a platform for people to share their viewpoints, ensuring that others hear and understand their message. This mutual understanding is essential for building strong connections and resolving conflicts. Trust is the foundation of any healthy relationship, and open communication is a cornerstone of trust.

When people communicate openly, it demonstrates transparency and sincerity. Trust is nurtured when individuals feel that they can rely on each other to communicate truthfully and openly about their thoughts and emotions. Conflicts are a natural part of life, but open communication is key to resolving them effectively.

When conflicts arise, open communication allows parties to express their concerns, identify the root causes of the conflict, and work together to find solutions and compromises. Avoiding communication during conflicts can lead to resentment and unresolved issues. People have a wide range of emotions, and open communication provides a safe space for the expression of these emotions.

It allows individuals to share their joys, fears, frustrations, and vulnerabilities. This emotional expression fosters a deeper connection and empathy among individuals. Open communication encourages personal and interpersonal growth. It enables individuals to provide and receive feedback, share insights, and learn from each other's experiences.

Constructive feedback helps individuals identify areas for improvement and make positive changes. In professional settings, open communication is essential for effective problem-solving and decision-making. Teams that communicate openly can collaborate more efficiently, brainstorm ideas, and reach consensus on solutions. This leads to better outcomes and productivity.

Open communication is key to building and maintaining strong, meaningful bonds in romantic relationships, friendships, or family connections. It fosters closeness, intimacy, and a sense of connection that strengthens over time. Misunderstandings can arise when communication is unclear, or assumptions are made.

Open communication reduces the likelihood of misinterpretations and ensures that information is conveyed accurately. It promotes active listening, clarifying doubts, and seeking clarification when needed. Open communication is rooted in respect for others' thoughts, feelings, and perspectives.

It demonstrates that individuals value and care about the people they are communicating with, leading to more respectful and considerate interactions. When individuals feel free to communicate openly, they are more likely to be their authentic selves. This authenticity fosters genuine connections and allows people to be accepted for who they truly are.

Constructive criticism is a valuable tool for personal and relationship growth. It's important to approach feedback to improve oneself and the relationship rather than viewing it as an attack. When an individual provides constructive criticism, it's a sign that they care about your growth and the health of the relationship.

Instead of becoming defensive, consider their perspective and see it as an opportunity to learn and grow together. In conclusion, expressing expectations is essential to building and maintaining healthy, meaningful relationships. Clear communication about roles and responsibilities fosters trust and reduces conflicts.

Admitting fault, when necessary, demonstrates humility and a commitment to growth. Open communication in any relationship allows two people to express themselves and receive feedback constructively. By embracing these principles, individuals can lay the foundation for a strong, enduring friendship or relationship filled with love, understanding, and growth.

CHAPTER 4

UNEQUALLY YOKED

I don't believe the phrase unequally yoked refers to color, race, or social status as opposed to a belief system, likes /dislikes, and lifestyles. It is essential to seek a mate with similar likes /dislikes, a similar belief system, and lifestyle.

I believe unequally yoked refers to, more specifically, where a person is spiritually, do they share the same religious beliefs that the person they desire to marry does. Are there any other differences that they have that could potentially prevent the union from being a success?

"Unequally yoked" is often associated with the idea that two individuals in a relationship are not well-matched or compatible in crucial aspects of their lives. I believe it primarily pertains to differences in belief systems, likes, dislikes, and lifestyles. Shared values and belief systems play a pivotal role in the success and compatibility of two individuals.

When two people have congruent values and beliefs, it creates a strong foundation for understanding, trust, and harmony. Shared values build trust between individuals because they know they can rely on each other to uphold the same principles. People with common values are more likely to respect each other's perspectives and decisions.

Common beliefs can create a deep emotional connection as individuals feel that they truly understand each other. People with shared values are less likely to have frequent conflicts and disagreements about fundamental issues. When conflicts do arise, having shared values can make it easier to find mutually acceptable solutions.

People with similar values tend to have aligned life goals, such as career aspirations, family planning, and financial priorities. Common values contribute to long-term compatibility, reducing the likelihood of one person feeling unfulfilled or unsupported. Shared values can provide emotional support during challenging times, as individuals can lean on each other for understanding and encouragement.

People who share beliefs often feel a stronger sense of belonging and unity, which can enhance their overall well-being. Those who share values can encourage each other's personal growth and development, as they have similar visions of what constitutes growth. Seeing each other live according to shared values can be inspiring and motivating.

When individuals share values and beliefs, they are better equipped to provide a consistent and unified approach to parenting. Parents with aligned values can effectively pass on their beliefs and moral principles to their children. For those who value spirituality or religion, shared beliefs can provide a profound sense of spiritual fulfillment and connection.

Individuals with shared spiritual beliefs often engage in meaningful customs and practices together, enhancing their bond. Shared values build trust and emotional intimacy in the relationship, as people are less likely to feel betrayed or misunderstood. Individuals may feel more comfortable being vulnerable with each other, knowing they are on the same page when it comes to their values.

Shared values can lead to a shared social circle with like-minded individuals, which can strengthen their sense of community. This shared community can serve as a support network for the relationship, offering guidance and validation. Similar likes and dislikes, such as hobbies and interests, can also significantly impact the quality and compatibility of a relationship.

While they may seem less critical than shared values and belief systems, they play an essential role in fostering connection, bonding, and long-term satisfaction in a relationship. Shared interests provide a natural foundation for bonding and spending quality time together. Engaging in activities both individuals enjoy can enhance the sense of togetherness and companionship.

Sharing hobbies or interests can improve communication within the relationship. It gives people more to talk about and fosters open and engaging conversations. People with similar likes often find spending meaningful and enjoyable time together easier. Whether it's watching the same movies, playing sports, or pursuing shared hobbies, these activities can create cherished lifelong memories.

Common interests can lead to shared goals and aspirations. For example, individuals who love hiking may set goals to explore specific trails or mountains together, fostering a sense of adventure and teamwork. Having shared interests can help prevent boredom and monotony in the relationship.

It ensures that there are always enjoyable activities to look forward to. Engaging in activities you both love can deepen the emotional connection between the two of you. The joy and satisfaction of shared experiences can translate into stronger emotional bonds. Similar likes and dislikes can extend beyond the two of you and influence your social life.

Individuals can often share friends with similar interests, leading to a vibrant and active social circle. Exploring new interests or hobbies together can be a fun and educational experience. It allows both people to learn and grow, both individually and together. People with shared interests are more likely to enjoy their leisure time together.

This alignment in leisure preferences can contribute to overall relationship satisfaction.

Having shared interests can provide a basis for resolving conflicts or disagreements. For example, when choosing activities, people can prioritize those activities they both enjoy in order to reach a compromise. Compatibility in likes and dislikes is not only about present enjoyment but also about long-term compatibility.

As individuals evolve, their interests may change, but having shared interests provides a flexible foundation for adaptation. Shared interests can become part of the individual's identity, reinforcing their bond and sense of belonging. Lifestyle compatibility is a crucial aspect of any successful and fulfilling relationship.

It refers to the degree to which two individuals' lifestyles align in terms of their daily routines, preferences, priorities, and long-term goals. A high level of lifestyle compatibility can contribute to the relationship's harmony, satisfaction, and longevity. People with compatible lifestyles tend to experience fewer conflicts related to daily routines and habits.

They are less likely to clash over issues like sleep patterns, cleanliness, or spending habits. Lifestyle compatibility often involves sharing similar priorities and goals. For example, both individuals may prioritize a healthy lifestyle, career advancement, or family planning, which can lead to smoother decision-making.

Those with compatible lifestyles are more likely to allocate their time in a way that satisfies both individuals. They can find a balance between personal pursuits, work, family, and leisure activities. Individuals with similar lifestyles tend to enjoy the same leisure activities, making it easier to spend quality time together.

Whether it's traveling, cooking, or pursuing hobbies, shared interests enhance the relationship.

Financial habits and values are an integral part of lifestyle compatibility. People who are on the same page regarding money matters are less likely to experience financial stress or disagreements.

Shared daily routines and lifestyle choices can deepen the emotional connection between people. Simple acts like cooking together, going for regular walks, or sharing morning activities can strengthen the connection between two individuals. Compatible lifestyles can facilitate personal growth for both individuals.

They can support each other's career ambitions, hobbies, and self-improvement goals. When people have compatible lifestyles, integrating their families and social circles into their relationships is often easier. This can lead to a more harmonious extended network. People with similar long-term goals, such as retirement plans, home ownership, or travel aspirations, are more likely to stay together and work towards these goals.

A shared commitment to a healthy lifestyle, including diet and exercise, can lead to better physical and mental well-being for both individuals. Lifestyle compatibility can reduce the need for constant communication about daily logistics. Individuals who understand each other's routines and can anticipate each other's needs.

During the early years of adulthood, individuals are in the process of forming their identities and values. The choices made during this period can have a profound and lasting impact on their viewpoints and preferences. Therefore, paying close attention to these aspects is crucial when evaluating a potential mate.

What may seem like minor differences in beliefs or lifestyles at the outset can grow into significant sources of conflict over time. If you frequently argue or disagree over fundamental values or preferences, it may be a sign of being unequally yoked. If you often feel unfulfilled or unsatisfied in the relationship, despite your significant other's good qualities, it could be due to differences in core values or lifestyle choices.

A lack of shared interests or hobbies can lead to a sense of disconnection and isolation within the relationship. Unresolved differences can breed resentment and frustration over time, eroding the emotional connection between two individuals. If you notice that you and your significant other are growing emotionally distant, it may be a consequence of being unequally yoked.

Being unequally yoked can trigger various character flaws and negative behaviors in both individuals. Feeling that your significant other's beliefs or choices invalidate your own can lead to feelings of insecurity. Resentment can build when one individual feels that their values or preferences are constantly overlooked or devalued.

Finding the balance between compromising for the sake of the relationship and sacrificing one's core values can be a challenging dilemma. Unequally yoked individuals may struggle with effective communication, as they often fail to understand each other's perspectives. In some cases, people may feel that they are unable to grow and evolve as individuals within the constraints of the relationship.

Being unequally yoked in a relationship refers to a misalignment in crucial aspects of life, including beliefs, likes, dislikes, and lifestyles. Recognizing the signs of being unequally yoked is essential for maintaining a healthy and fulfilling relationship. Additionally, understanding the effects of being unequally yoked and the impact that it can have on your life and relationship decisions will benefit you for years to come.

CHAPTER 5

CHOOSING A MATE

In order to be able to choose a mate, you first have to have an understanding of what you desire both for yourself and the person you desire to marry. Knowledge of self is very important to have a healthy relationship and marriage. Although no one knows everything about themselves, and feelings change at times, it's important to make an attempt to get to know the essence of who you are and where you desire to go in life.

Being in tune with yourself, your likes, dislikes, and tolerances is very instrumental in making wise relationship choices. In a relationship each person should have respect enough for the other to allow each other to speak openly and honestly about their feelings. It is important to remember that each party has a voice in the relationship and that it is important to listen to each other.

Listening can be difficult when the person that you are talking to is immature or prideful. To block out a person who means well for you and is trying to help the two of you be better should be a red flag and could be the beginning of the end of your relationship. It is important that each person's voice or thoughts are heard even though you may not always agree, but at least you listen to hear each other out.

Choosing a life partner is one of the most significant decisions a person can make in their lifetime. It's a decision that can shape the course of your life, influencing your happiness, personal growth, and overall well-being. Before embarking on the journey of choosing a mate, it's essential to have a deep understanding of yourself and your desires.

Self-awareness and self-knowledge are the cornerstones of making wise decisions in relationships. Taking the time to reflect on your core values and life goals is instrumental. What matters most to you in life? Knowing your values helps you seek a partner who shares similar principles.

Reflecting on your likes and dislikes, including your hobbies, interests, and lifestyle preferences, as well as understanding what brings you joy and fulfillment, is essential in finding a compatible partner. It's essential to be able to recognize your boundaries and tolerances in a relationship. What are the things you are willing to accept, and what will you not accept?

Self-awareness helps you establish healthy boundaries. Emotional self-awareness is vital. Understanding your emotions and how you respond to them can help you navigate the challenges and joys of a relationship more effectively. Reflecting on past relationships and the lessons you've learned from them will hopefully prevent you from making repetitive mistakes.

Your previous experiences can provide valuable insights into what you're looking for in a partner.

Before embarking on the journey of selecting a mate, it is crucial to have a deep understanding of yourself and your desires. Self-awareness is the foundation upon which successful relationships can be built. Taking time to reflect on your core values, beliefs, and life goals can assist you in your self-awareness. What are the things that matter most to you?

Knowing your values helps you align with a partner who shares similar principles. Being able to identify your boundaries and tolerances in a relationship will help you be able to discuss your position on various concerns and make you more aware of where you are emotionally and physically.

What are things you will not accept, and what will you compromise on? This self-awareness can guide you in selecting the right mate. Being attuned to your own emotions and how you handle them can prevent emotional meltdowns in times of stress and disagreements. Emotions can significantly impact your relationships, and knowing how to manage them is crucial.

Once you understand yourself better, setting standards for the type of relationship you desire is essential. This involves evaluating potential mates by these standards. Knowing what you will not accept or not compromise on is crucial to choosing a mate and building a healthy and fulfilling relationship.

Understanding what you will refuse to accept helps you form a relationship standard and assists you in making informed decisions about whom to pursue as a mate. Identifying what you will not accept or not compromise on provides clarity about what you truly desire in a mate; it helps you distinguish between what you're willing to accept and what you're not willing to accept. This is a reflection of your self-respect and self-worth. It demonstrates that you value yourself enough to establish boundaries and expectations in a relationship. Knowing what you will and will not accept helps you avoid entering into relationships that are unlikely to fulfill your needs and desires. It reduces the risk of settling for less than you deserve.

It protects your emotional well-being. Adhering to your standards can prevent situations that may lead to emotional turmoil or unhappiness. When you are clear on what you will and will not accept, you can quickly assess whether a potential mate aligns with your values and desires. This streamlines the decision-making process and can serve as boundaries in a relationship.

It communicates to your mate what is acceptable and what is not, which can lead to healthier dynamics. It can also vary from person to person, as they are deeply personal and reflective of individual values and priorities. Being transparent with what you will or will not accept for many people is mutual respect.

They may require that their mate always treats them with kindness and respect, and disrespectful behavior will not be tolerated. Some individuals may insist on complete honesty and trustworthiness in their mate, unwilling to tolerate lies or deceit. Engaging in open and honest communication will hopefully foster open and honest communication within the relationship. For some, it is a must to be able to share fundamental values like religious beliefs, moral principles, or life goals. Other individuals may require a mate who shares their ambitions and long-term goals, such as career aspirations, family planning, health, and well-being (which can include maintaining a healthy lifestyle or seeking medical attention when necessary) and financial compatibility, which includes sharing views of money management.

It's important to note that what you will and will not accept may evolve as your values, priorities, and life circumstances change. Regular self-reflection and open communication with your mate can help ensure that you remain aligned with your current needs and desires. Be honest with yourself about your desires and expectations. Setting unrealistic expectations can lead to disappointment and frustration in a relationship.

It's essential not to settle for a mate who doesn't meet your standards or who doesn't align with your values. Settling for less can lead to dissatisfaction and unhappiness in the long run. Look for compatibility in areas such as values, interests, communication styles, and long-term goals. Compatibility is a strong indicator of relationship success.

Respect is a cornerstone of any healthy and thriving relationship. It involves recognizing the worth and autonomy of both you and your mate. In a respectful relationship, both individuals acknowledge that each person has a voice, thoughts, and opinions that are important. Listening to each other is key to mutual respect.

Respect entails open and honest communication where both individuals feel safe expressing their thoughts and feelings without fear of judgment or ridicule. Immaturity and pride can hinder respectful communication. It's essential to recognize when these behaviors arise and work on addressing them for the sake of the relationship.

Disrespect in a relationship can lead to a breakdown of trust, emotional distance, and resentment. It can erode the connection between individuals and create a hostile environment. Even when you disagree, respecting each other's perspectives is vital. It's possible to have differing opinions while still respecting one another.

Active listening involves not just hearing but truly understanding your mates' points of view. It shows that you value and respect their thoughts. Respect includes empathy and compassion for your mates' feelings and experiences. It means being there for them during both joyous and challenging times.

A respectful relationship builds trust over time. Trust is essential for emotional intimacy and the overall health of the relationship. When respect is present, both individuals have the space and support to grow individually and as a couple. It fosters an environment of growth and improvement.

Choosing a mate is a significant decision that requires self-awareness, self-evaluation, and a commitment to mutual respect. Understanding your own values and desires, setting standards, and seeking compatibility are essential steps in this process. Moreover, respect is the foundation of a healthy relationship, fostering open communication, trust, and emotional connection. Individuals can make informed choices and build a lasting relationship by prioritizing these aspects.

CHAPTER 6

WHAT SEASON IS IT

Just as nature goes through cycles of change, relationships experience different phases and seasons. Understanding these relationship seasons can help you conduct yourselves appropriately, navigate challenges, and prepare for what lies ahead. Relationships are just like the seasons of the year; you go through a spring where there is new life and excitement, a summer where things are in full bloom, a fall where things are cooling off, and a winter where things may seem dead and nonexistent.

Much like the season of spring, the early stages of a relationship are characterized by new beginnings and growth.

During this season, the foundation of trust and open communication should be established. Nurture the trust between you and your partner, as it forms the roots of a healthy relationship.

Allow yourself to be excited about the newness of the relationship. Explore shared interests, discover each other's quirks, and enjoy the blossoming connection. Recognize that, like spring flowers, relationships take time to bloom fully. Be patient and give your connection the time it needs to grow.

Understand that even in spring, there can be rainy days. In relationships, expect minor disagreements or challenges and be prepared to handle them with understanding and compromise.

Summer in relationships is when things are in full bloom, and you're enjoying the peak of your connection.

Continue to nurture your relationship as you care for a flourishing garden in summer. Spend quality time together and celebrate your shared achievements. As you maintain open and honest communication, share your thoughts, feelings, and desires to ensure your connection remains strong. Celebrate your partner's successes and milestones. A thriving relationship thrives on mutual support and celebration.

In summer, there's the risk of overheating. In relationships, this can manifest as excessive conflicts or burnout. Practice self-care and ensure you maintain a balance in your lives.

Just as autumn brings cooler weather and falling leaves, the fall season in a relationship is marked by transitions and changes.

Understand that change is a natural part of any relationship. Be adaptable and open to the transitions that come your way. Use this season as an opportunity to reflect on the relationship. What has worked well? What might need adjustment or improvement? Just as leaves fall in autumn, you may face challenges in your relationship.

Be prepared to address these challenges with patience and empathy. As the days grow shorter, prioritize self-care to ensure you and your partner remain emotionally healthy and resilient.

Winter is a season of rest and renewal in nature, and similarly, in relationships, it can be a time for reflection and self-care.

Allow your relationship some downtime. This could be a period of less activity or even a brief break if needed. Reflect on the relationship's journey so far and reconnect with your partner. Use this time to deepen your emotional bond. Just as nature prepares for the upcoming spring, use the winter season to plan for your relationship's future. Discuss goals, dreams, and aspirations.

Although winter can be cold, it's important to maintain emotional warmth in your relationship. Show appreciation and affection to your partner. In both nature and relationships, change is inevitable. Seasons transition, and so does your life and the dynamics of your relationships. To ensure the longevity and resilience of a relationship, it's essential to prepare for the next season, anticipating and embracing the changes that lie ahead.

Here are some key strategies for preparing for the next season in your relationship.

Effective communication is the foundation of any successful relationship, especially when it comes to anticipating and managing change. To prepare for the next season, continue to communicate openly and honestly with your partner. Discuss your expectations, dreams, and concerns about the future.

Take the time to discuss your individual and shared expectations for the relationship's next season. What are your short-term and long-term goals as a couple? Do you have any specific plans or aspirations? Being on the same page about your relationship's direction is crucial for a smooth transition.

Reflect on the past seasons of your relationship and the lessons you've learned along the way. What worked well in previous transitions, and what challenges did you face? By acknowledging past experiences, you can make more informed decisions about how to navigate the future. Change often requires flexibility and adaptability.

Be prepared to adjust your approach or expectations as your relationship evolves. Being rigid or resistant to change can lead to unnecessary stress and conflict. Instead, adopt a mindset of flexibility to navigate transitions more smoothly. Identify and set mutual goals for the relationship's next season. What do you want to achieve together?

These goals could relate to personal growth, shared experiences, career aspirations, or family planning. Establishing common objectives can create a sense of purpose and direction. Just as you nurture a garden year-round to prepare for the next growing season, continue to invest in your relationship.

Maintain your emotional connection, spend quality time together, and engage in activities that strengthen your bond. Regularly check in with each other to ensure you're both on the same page. While focusing on the growth of your relationship, also pay attention to your individual growth and development.

Personal growth can positively impact the relationship as both individuals continue to evolve and bring new perspectives to the partnership. Change is not always easy, but it can be an opportunity for growth, learning, and new experiences. Embrace change as a chance to strengthen your relationship, adapt to new circumstances, and overcome challenges together. Remember that growth often occurs outside of your comfort zone. Preparing for the next season in your relationship requires emotional resilience and self-care. Take care of your physical and mental well-being to ensure you have the energy and emotional capacity to navigate change effectively. Self-care includes activities like exercise, mindfulness, and seeking support when needed.

Approach the next season in your relationship with a positive outlook. Believe in your ability as a couple to face challenges and make the necessary adjustments. A positive attitude can be a driving force in navigating change successfully. Finally, take a moment to celebrate the journey you've been on together.

Reflect on the progress you've made as a couple and the obstacles you've overcome. Celebrating the achievements and growth can strengthen your connection and build confidence as you face the future. Just as spring represents new beginnings and growth, summer symbolizes the flourishing of love and connection.

You experience transitions and changes in the fall, and winter offers you a time for rest and reflection. Recognizing the season your relationship is in allows you to respond appropriately and adapt to the evolving dynamics. Open and honest communication is the foundation of a successful relationship.

Whether you're basking in summer's warmth or facing autumn's challenges, effective communication is key to understanding and supporting each other. Relationships require flexibility and adaptability. Having a willingness to adjust and compromise as you move through different seasons can help you weather the storms and enjoy the sunny days together.

Just as nature rebounds from the harshest of winters, relationships can overcome difficulties when individuals are committed and resilient. Resilience means facing challenges head-on and working together to find solutions. Every season in a relationship offers an opportunity for personal and collective growth.

Whether you're nurturing a budding connection in the spring or deepening your bond in the summer, growth is a continual process. Love and respect should be present in all seasons. Treating each other with kindness, empathy, and respect is the cornerstone of a healthy and lasting relationship.

As you navigate the seasons of your relationship, remember that change is a constant, but with understanding, patience, and a willingness to adapt, you can create a relationship that survives and thrives in every season. By embracing the beauty of each season and learning from the challenges they bring, you can build a loving relationship that is as enduring and resilient as the cycles of nature.

Understanding that relationships, like nature's seasons, go through distinct phases and is crucial for building and maintaining a healthy and fulfilling partnership. Each season brings unique challenges and opportunities, and navigating these seasons can significantly impact your life.

CHAPTER 7

THE CHOICE IS YOURS

In this journey, you call life, one of the most crucial decisions you will make is choosing the right person to share it with. This choice can profoundly impact your future, and it's essential to approach it with care, patience, and self-awareness. It is important to make the correct choice when it comes to relationships.

Transparency with oneself and others can spare you from heartache, headaches, and a lifetime of regret. Being with someone can change the trajectory of your life for the good or for the bad, depending on how and who you choose. Some people choose the right person to spend the rest of their life with without hesitation or questions.

Others tend to have a more difficult road to relationship happiness, especially when choosing an appropriate mate for themselves. Again, knowledge of self is vital in the selection process, and knowing what you can put up with and what you cannot is equally important. Patience is also important, and knowing that preparing oneself for the right person is key.

Working to improve your character flaws is vital, and admitting that you have deficiencies is also important. Depending on your choices, being with someone can alter your life's course, either for the better or worse. Some people are fortunate enough to find the right mate easily, while others face a more challenging journey towards relationship happiness.

The key to a successful choice lies in self-awareness, understanding your own needs, and recognizing what you can and cannot tolerate in a mate. The power of choosing wisely in relationships cannot be overstated. The decision of who you choose as a mate can have a profound and lasting impact on your life.

A healthy, loving relationship can greatly enhance your overall quality of life. It can provide emotional support, companionship, and happiness. On the other hand, choosing the wrong mate can lead to stress, conflict, and unhappiness. A good mate can inspire personal growth and self-improvement. They can encourage you to be your best self and achieve your goals.

Conversely, a toxic or incompatible mate can hold you back and hinder your personal development. Being with the right person can contribute to your emotional well-being. It can provide a sense of security and belonging. A toxic relationship, on the other hand, can lead to emotional turmoil, anxiety, and even depression.

Your mate should be your biggest supporter. You should be there for them in times of need and celebrate their successes. Choosing a supportive mate can make life's challenges more manageable. Compatibility in values, goals, and interests is essential for a successful relationship. Choosing someone who shares your core values and life objectives can lead to a harmonious and fulfilling relationship.

Furthermore, a well-thought-out and intentional choice when it comes to marriage or any long-term relationship is crucial for building a lasting and enduring relationship. In addition, mutual respect, trust, and love are important in maintaining a strong relationship. Effective and open communication is the foundation of any healthy relationship.

It's essential to express your thoughts, feelings, and concerns honestly and to listen to your mate with empathy. Mutual respect involves valuing each other's opinions, boundaries, and individuality. It's about treating your mate with kindness and consideration. Trust is the foundation of a strong relationship.

It's built over time through reliability, honesty, and consistency in your actions and words. Trust allows you to feel safe and secure in the relationship. Love is the emotional glue that binds couples together. It's not just romantic love but also the love that comes from deep friendship and understanding. Love is nurtured through care, affection, and support.

Life is filled with changes and challenges. Successful relationships are those that can adapt to these changes and work together to overcome difficulties. Spending quality time together is essential for maintaining a strong connection. It's not just about being physically present but being emotionally present and engaged.

Disagreements are inevitable in any relationship, but how you handle them matters. Healthy conflict resolution involves listening, compromise, and finding solutions together. Couples with common goals and visions for the future tend to have a more enduring relationship. It's important to regularly revisit and update your goals as a couple.

Emotional intimacy is a vital part of a romantic relationship. It's important to nurture the emotional connection between two individuals. Supporting each other's personal growth and development is essential. It's important to encourage your mate to pursue their interests and dreams.

Regularly express your appreciation for your mate. Small gestures of gratitude can go a long way in strengthening a relationship. Mistakes and misunderstandings happen. Forgiving and letting go of past grievances is vital for moving forward. A well-balanced, loving, and respectful relationship is an ongoing process that requires effort from both individuals.

It's about continually investing in the relationship, adapting to change, and nurturing the emotional connection. Both individuals are more likely to enjoy a long-lasting and enduring relationship when they are committed to these principles. If you plan to have a family, your choice of a mate becomes even more critical.

The person you choose will influence the upbringing and well-being of your children. It's essential to select someone who aligns with your parenting values. Financial compatibility is another crucial aspect. Choosing someone who shares your financial goals and is responsible with money can help avoid conflicts and financial stress in the future.

A wise choice in choosing a mate can provide peace of mind. You'll have confidence that your mate has your best interests at heart, and you won't have to constantly worry about the stability of your relationship. Ultimately, the power of choosing wisely in relationships lies in the potential for happiness. A loving, healthy relationship can bring immense joy and contentment to your life.

To make a wise choice in a mate, it's important to take your time, get to know the person, communicate openly, and trust your instincts. Don't rush into a relationship or ignore red flags. Remember that it's better to be single than to be in an unhealthy or incompatible relationship. Your happiness and well-being are worth the effort it takes to choose wisely.

Before choosing the right person for your life, one must know oneself. Self-awareness is the foundation upon which healthy relationships are built. Understand your values, your aspirations, and your boundaries. Recognize your strengths and weaknesses. Knowing what makes you happy and what makes you thrive is essential in making an informed choice.

Rushing into a relationship can be a recipe for disaster. Patience is your ally when it comes to finding the right person. Don't settle for less than you deserve, and don't force a connection when it's not genuine. Sometimes, waiting for the right person to come into your life is the best decision one can make.

No one is perfect, and acknowledging your imperfections is crucial to making the right choice. Work on improving yourself and addressing your character flaws. Be open to growth and change. Remember that a successful relationship requires effort from both individuals and being the best version of yourselves will benefit both.

In the process of choosing a life companion, honesty and transparency are your allies. Be transparent with your potential companion about your intentions, your values, and your expectations. Equally important, be honest with yourself about what you want and need in a relationship.

Avoid hiding your true self or pretending to be someone you're not, as this can only lead to misunderstandings and disappointment later on. Transparency is a fundamental aspect of any healthy and successful relationship, whether it's a romantic relationship, a friendship, a family bond, or a professional collaboration.

Trust is the foundation of any strong relationship. Transparency involves being open, honest, and truthful with one another. When you consistently demonstrate transparency, it helps build trust, as it shows that you have nothing to hide. Transparent communication encourages open and constructive dialogue.

Sharing your thoughts, feelings, and concerns openly allows others to do the same. This paves the way for effective communication, problem-solving, and conflict resolution. Lack of transparency can lead to misunderstandings and misinterpretations. When you are clear and honest about your intentions, expectations, and boundaries, it reduces the likelihood of confusion and conflict.

Sharing your true self, including your vulnerabilities and insecurities, can help deepen emotional connections in relationships. Being transparent about your emotions allows others to empathize and connect with you on a deeper level. Transparency encourages accountability for one's actions and decisions.

When you're open about your choices and their consequences, it becomes easier to take responsibility for them and make necessary adjustments. Authenticity is about being your true self and not pretending to be someone you're not. Transparency is key to authenticity, as it involves revealing your genuine thoughts, feelings, and intentions.

In times of conflict, transparency is crucial. It helps address the conflict's root causes and find mutually agreeable solutions. Trying to hide or manipulate information during a conflict can escalate the situation. Transparent relationships tend to be more stable in the long run. When both individuals are open and honest with each other, it reduces the risk of hidden issues surfacing later and causing irreparable damage to the relationship.

Being transparent with someone is a sign of respect and consideration. It shows that you value the other person enough to be honest with them, even when the truth may be uncomfortable. Transparency helps establish and maintain healthy boundaries in relationships. When you communicate your boundaries clearly, it allows others to understand and respect them.

In some cases, transparency can prevent conflicts from arising in the first place. When you proactively share important information and make your intentions clear, it reduces the chances of misunderstandings and disagreements. Being transparent with others can also promote personal growth.

Sharing your goals, aspirations, and areas where you're working on self-improvement can invite support and encouragement from those around you. The path to self-improvement is a personal journey of growth and development that can lead to a more fulfilling and meaningful life. It involves a deliberate effort to become the best version of yourself.

Take the time to reflect on your strengths, weaknesses, values, and goals. Understand your motivations, fears, and desires. This self-awareness serves as a foundation for growth. These goals could be related to your personal life, career, relationships, or health. Having clear objectives provides direction and motivation.

Seek out opportunities to acquire additional knowledge, skills, and experiences. Continuous learning is essential for personal growth, whether through formal education, workshops, books, or online courses. Don't shy away from challenges or failures; embrace them as opportunities to learn and develop resilience.

Each setback can be a stepping stone toward improvement. Develop self-discipline and self-control; this involves setting priorities, managing your time effectively, and making choices that align with your goals. It also includes the ability to delay gratification for long-term benefits.

Cultivate healthy habits that support your physical and mental well-being.

This includes regular exercise, a balanced diet, sufficient sleep, and stress management techniques like meditation or mindfulness. Be open to feedback from others. Constructive feedback can provide valuable insights into areas where you can improve. Listen to feedback with an open mind and use it as a tool for growth.

Life is constantly changing, and adaptability is a key skill for self-improvement. Embrace change as an opportunity for growth and be willing to adjust your goals and strategies as needed. Resilience is the ability to face challenges with strength and determination rather than being overwhelmed by them.

Cultivate a positive mindset. Focus on your strengths and achievements, and practice self-compassion. Replace negative self-talk with positive affirmations and thoughts.

Regularly assess your progress and make adjustments as necessary. Celebrate your successes, learn from your failures, and continue refining successes, learn your goals and strategies.

Surround yourself with positive influences and seek inspiration from mentors, role models, or those who have achieved what you aspire to. Learning from others can accelerate your self-improvement journey. Self-improvement is a lifelong journey, and it requires patience and persistence.

Understand that meaningful change takes time, and setbacks are part of the process. You will provide valuable insight into the nature of your self-improvement. Self-improvement is indeed a lifelong journey that demands patience and persistence. Real and lasting change doesn't happen overnight.

It's important to be patient with yourself and your progress. Acknowledge that improvement takes time. Everyone encounters setbacks and obstacles on the path to self-improvement. These setbacks are part of the process, not failures. Learn from them and use them as opportunities for growth.

Staying committed to your personal growth is essential. It requires dedication and a willingness to put in the effort to become the best version of yourself. Be open to adjusting your goals and strategies as you learn and grow. What you initially set out to achieve may change as you gain new insights and experiences.

Consistency is key to making meaningful progress. Small, consistent efforts over time can lead to significant positive changes. Regularly take the time to reflect on your goals, values, and progress. Self-reflection helps you stay on course and make necessary adjustments. Don't hesitate to seek support from mentors, friends, or resources that can aid in your self-improvement journey.

By embracing these principles and understanding that self-improvement is a long-term commitment, you can work towards becoming the best version of yourself. It's a rewarding journey that leads to personal growth, increased self-awareness, and a more fulfilling life. The choice of a life companion is one of the most important decisions you'll ever make.

Take the time to know yourself, be patient in your search, work on self-improvement, and prioritize transparency in your interactions. Doing so increases your chances of choosing the right person to share your life with and avoid a lifetime of regret. Remember, the choice is yours, and it's worth choosing wisely.

"The choice is yours" encapsulates the fundamental principle that your life is shaped by the decisions you make. Whether it's choosing a lifelong companion, embarking on a journey of self-improvement, or making any significant life choice, the power to decide rests with us. Ultimately, understanding that "the choice is yours" empowers individuals to make decisions that lead to a more fulfilling and purposeful life.

It serves as a reminder that your choices can shape your futures and that you should approach them with care, consideration, and a commitment to your well-being and happiness.

CHAPTER 8

MARRIAGE

Marriage is a profound institution that can bring numerous benefits and rewards when entered into with careful consideration and commitment. It signifies a union between two individuals, marked by love, partnership, and a promise to support one another through life's joys and challenges. However, it is essential to recognize that marrying the wrong person can have adverse effects on both the individuals involved and the marriage itself.

Marriage helps to shield you from unwanted and unfruitful advances or relationships. It is not a cure-all for these issues, but it can serve as a deterrent. It's a source of protection from storms that may come your way because it's two fighting together instead of one fighting alone. However, when married to the wrong person, it can be a place of regret, bondage, frustration, and exhaustion.

Marriage can protect you from wrong relationships. Wrong meaning, relationships that should not be engaged in, relationships that are detrimental to your marriage's health. It helps one stay focused and consistent with your purpose and goals (when your spouse is supportive and appreciative of your efforts).

It's a one-way street where two people travel together with love, compassion, understanding and respect. Marriage helps you grow and mature individually and collectively by the side of another individual. Individually, it forces you to look at yourselves and gives your spouse the freedom to tell you about your character flaws in order to help you become better versions of yourselves.

Becoming a better version of yourselves should be vital to personal growth and maturity.

Marriage can be messy and painful at times, but it allows two people to work through the pain and mess to bring healing and order. Building a strong foundation in a marriage is crucial for its long-term success and happiness. Respect is the foundation upon which trust and love are built. Treat your spouse with kindness, consideration, and appreciation. Value their opinions, feelings, and boundaries.

Effective communication is at the heart of any thriving marriage. Share your thoughts, feelings, and concerns openly and honestly. Listen actively to your partner without judgment or defensiveness. It's essential to align your values and long-term goals. Discuss your aspirations, whether they relate to career, family, or personal growth, and find common ground to work toward together.

Emotional intimacy involves connecting on a deep emotional level. Share your vulnerabilities, fears, and dreams with your spouse. Create a safe space where both individuals can express themselves without fear of judgment. Spend quality time together regularly. This includes enjoying shared activities, date nights, and simply being present with each other.

Quality time strengthens the emotional connection of your relationship. Trust is the foundation of any successful marriage. Be transparent and consistent in your actions and words. Keep your promises and avoid deceit or betrayal. Disagreements are a part of relationships. Learn how to resolve conflicts constructively, focusing on finding solutions rather than assigning blame.

Avoid escalating arguments and practice active listening. While being a team is crucial, it's also essential to maintain your individual identities and interests. Encourage each other to pursue personal passions and maintain a sense of self. Clearly define roles and responsibilities in your marriage, including chores, finances, and childcare, if applicable.

Fairly distribute these responsibilities to avoid feelings of inequality or resentment. Life is full of changes and challenges. Be adaptable and willing to adjust to new circumstances involving career changes, family dynamics, or other unexpected events. Be each other's biggest cheerleaders.

Support your spouse's dreams and ambitions, providing encouragement and motivation along the way. Take the time to regularly assess and discuss the state of your marriage. This can help you identify areas needing improvement and make necessary adjustments sooner. If you encounter significant challenges or unresolved issues, don't hesitate to seek the guidance of a marriage counselor or therapist.

Professional help can provide valuable tools and insights. Building a strong foundation in marriage is an ongoing process that requires effort and commitment from both individuals. By prioritizing these elements and continually working on your relationship, one can create a loving, resilient, and fulfilling marriage that stands the test of time.

Marriage offers a deep emotional connection and support system. Having a life companion can provide a sense of security, companionship, and someone to confide in during difficult times. Individuals tend to have better physical and mental health when they have the emotional support and encouragement of a committed marriage.

Shared financial responsibilities often lead to better financial planning and security. This can include joint savings, investments, and the pooling of resources. Marriage often leads to creating a family unit, which can be a source of joy and fulfillment. It also provides a social structure and a sense of belonging within a community.

It also grants certain legal rights and protections, including inheritance, medical decision-making, and tax benefits. Marrying the wrong person can have profound and lasting negative effects. Being in a relationship with the wrong person can cause chronic stress, anxiety, and emotional turmoil.

Continuously being with someone who doesn't value or appreciate can erode self-esteem and self-confidence. The wrong person can lead to poor communication, as both individuals may struggle to connect and understand each other. Unresolved issues and incompatibility can result in constant conflict and unhappiness within the marriage.

Marrying the wrong person can have significant and often detrimental impacts on both the individuals involved and the marriage itself. These consequences can manifest in various ways, leading to emotional, psychological, and even physical challenges.

Being in a marriage with the wrong person can result in ongoing emotional distress.

This might include feelings of sadness, anxiety, depression, or constant frustration. Incompatibility and fundamental differences in values or personality can lead to a breakdown in communication. Couples may struggle to understand each other or resolve conflicts effectively.

Marrying the wrong person often leads to frequent conflicts and overall unhappiness in the marriage.

These conflicts can range from minor disagreements to major, unresolved issues. Continuously being with someone who doesn't value or appreciates you can erode self-esteem and self-confidence. This can lead to feelings of inadequacy and self-doubt. In some cases, marrying the wrong person can lead to social isolation as individuals may withdraw from friends and family due to the stress and strain of the marriage.

If the wrong person is controlling or possessive, one may lose your sense of independence and autonomy in the marriage. Incompatible goals and values can lead to a sense of stagnation. You may find yourself unable to pursue your own aspirations or grow personally within the confines of marriage.

Over time, unresolved issues and unmet needs can breed resentment. This resentment can further poison the marriage, making it difficult to rebuild trust and connection. The chronic stress and emotional turmoil caused by being with the wrong person can lead to physical health problems like headaches, insomnia, and even more severe conditions.

It can also contribute to mental health issues such as anxiety and depression. If children are part of the marriage, they may be negatively affected by the discord and tension within the household. This can lead to emotional and developmental challenges for the children. In some cases, the realization that you've married the wrong person may lead to divorce or separation, which can be emotionally and financially taxing for both individuals.

It's essential to recognize the signs of being in a marriage with the wrong person early on and take appropriate steps to address the issues. This might involve seeking couples therapy or counseling, having open and honest conversations with your spouse, and, in some cases, making the difficult decision to end the marriage to pursue a healthier, more compatible relationship.

In the long run, prioritizing your well-being and happiness is crucial, even if it means confronting the challenging reality of marrying the wrong person. Growing and nurturing a marriage is an ongoing journey that requires both individuals' attention, effort, and dedication.

Engage in open and honest communication regularly.

Discuss your thoughts, feelings, and concerns with your spouse. Practice active listening, which means genuinely paying attention to what your spouse is saying without interrupting or preparing your response. Make time for each other amid the busyness of life. Schedule regular date nights or special activities that you both enjoy.

Disconnect from digital distractions during your quality time to fully focus on each other. Revisit shared interests and hobbies to strengthen your bond. Express your love and affection regularly.

Small gestures like hugs, kisses, and compliments can go a long way in nurturing emotional intimacy.

Physical touch is essential for many couples, so don't underestimate the power of holding hands or cuddling. Encourage your spouse's personal growth and aspirations. Be their biggest cheerleader and provide emotional support. Collaborate on setting shared goals and working together to achieve them, whether they are related to finances, family, or other areas of life.

Try to see things from your spouse's perspective. Empathize with their feelings and experiences, even if you don't always agree. Be patient and understanding when your spouse faces challenges or makes mistakes. Show that you're there to support them. Surprise each other with thoughtful gestures, gifts, or love notes. Spice up your intimate life by exploring new experiences and maintaining a healthy physical connection.

Disagreements are inevitable, but it's how one handles them that matters. Focus on finding solutions instead of dwelling on the problem. Practice active listening during conflicts, and use "we" language to emphasize that you're working together to resolve the issue. Trust is the foundation of any lasting relationship.

Be reliable and consistent in your actions and words. Avoid situations or behaviors that can erode trust, such as dishonesty or secrecy. While nurturing your marriage, remember to maintain your individual interests, friendships, and hobbies. This helps one maintain a sense of self and prevents codependency.

Don't hesitate to seek professional help, such as couples counseling or therapy, if you encounter challenges that are difficult to resolve on your own. Seeking outside guidance can provide valuable insights and strategies to strengthen your marriage. Acknowledge and celebrate important milestones and anniversaries in your marriage.

These moments serve as reminders of your shared life together. Understand that both you and your spouse will make mistakes. Practice forgiveness and patience as you navigate challenges together. Growing and nurturing a marriage is a continuous learning process, adapting and deepening your connection.

By prioritizing these strategies and working together as a team, you can cultivate a loving, resilient marriage that thrives over time. Making false promises in a marriage can be damaging. To avoid this, be realistic about what you can and cannot provide or change. Understand that no one is perfect, and no marriage is without flaws.

Instead of making grandiose promises, focus on being the best spouse so that you can consistently show love, respect, and support. Before getting married, there are several important things to consider and take care of. Both individuals should be genuinely committed to the idea of marriage and to each other.

Make sure you are both on the same page and have discussed your future together. Understand the legal requirements for marriage in your jurisdiction. This includes obtaining a marriage license, adhering to any waiting periods, submitting to blood tests, and meeting age requirements.

Having an open and honest conversation about your financial situation and future goals is essential. Discuss how you will manage finances, including budgeting, saving, and handling debts. Ensure that you and your future spouse have common values, beliefs, and long-term goals. This includes discussing issues like religion, family planning, culinary preferences, and career ambitions.

Strong communication is key to a successful marriage. Work on your communication skills to effectively express your needs and concerns and be a good listener. Learn how to handle conflicts and disagreements in a healthy and respectful manner. Consider pre-marital counseling or therapy if needed.

Have a support system in place, such as friends and family who are there for you. A strong social network can be valuable in times of need. Ensure that you and your future spouse have access to health insurance and consider discussing healthcare decisions, especially if you plan to start a family.

Discuss household and family responsibilities. Decide who will handle what, and make sure you're both comfortable with the division of labor. Consider legal documents like prenuptial agreements, wills, and power of attorney if they are relevant to your situation. Be emotionally prepared for the commitment that marriage entails.

Understand that there will be challenges and be willing to work through them together. Many couples find pre-marital counseling beneficial. It can help one address potential issues, improve communication, and strengthen your relationship prior to marriage. If you plan to have children, talk about your parenting styles, expectations, and timelines for starting a family.

Discuss where you plan to live and what type of housing arrangements you'll have after getting married. Talk about your travel aspirations and leisure activities. Ensure you have some common interests and ways to relax together. If applicable, consider any religious or cultural rituals or ceremonies associated with marriage and discuss how you'll incorporate them into your wedding.

Plan the type of wedding or marriage ceremony you desire and the celebrations that will follow.

It's important to remember that every relationship is unique, and the specific considerations may vary from one couple to another. Communication, trust, and mutual respect are key elements in preparing for a successful marriage. Don't hesitate to seek advice or counseling if you have concerns or doubts, as addressing issues before marriage can lead to a stronger and more fulfilling partnership.

Marriage is a complex and profound institution that can bring both immense joy and profound challenges to your life. It represents a commitment to love and support another person, and when entered into with care, consideration, and a dedication to growth, it can be one of the most rewarding aspects of life. Marriage offers numerous benefits, including emotional support, financial stability, and the opportunity to create a loving family.

However, it's important to recognize that marrying the wrong person can adversely affect your well-being and happiness. A healthy and successful marriage requires a strong foundation, continuous effort, and open communication. Building a strong foundation involves mutual respect, open and honest communication, shared values and goals, emotional intimacy, quality time together, trust, and the ability to resolve conflicts constructively.

It also requires individuality and the support of each other's personal growth. Nurturing a marriage involves ongoing efforts to maintain and deepen the connection between two individuals. This includes showing affection, supporting each other's goals, practicing empathy and understanding, keeping the romance alive, resolving conflicts, cultivating trust, maintaining individuality, and seeking help when needed.

Marriage will have ups and downs, but with dedication and commitment to these principles, couples can navigate challenges, celebrate milestones, and build a lasting and fulfilling marriage. Ultimately, a successful marriage is built on love, trust, and the willingness to grow and evolve together as individuals and as a couple.

CHAPTER 9

JUST SAY YES

Just say yes. I've heard people say that the best way to keep a happy marriage is to

"Just say yes." Whenever your spouse wants something, just say yes. I have to disagree with this philosophy. To love your spouse is to tell the truth, even if it is unpopular. No two people will agree on everything, but you can agree to disagree if need be.

Life is not about always getting what you want, nor is marriage. But it is about sharing, giving, and meeting your spouse right where they are. Understanding that decisions are made to support the marriage and accepting the hills and valleys of marriage is a major step to maturity and longevity.

In the world of marriage and relationships, there's an old adage that sometimes gets passed around: "Just say yes." The idea behind this saying is that saying yes to your spouse's requests or desires, whenever possible, can lead to a happier and more harmonious marriage. While this advice has good intentions, there's more to consider when making a marriage work.

Working together to make a marriage work is absolutely crucial for its success and longevity. A strong and healthy marriage is a relationship in which both spouses collaborate, communicate, and support each other. A successful marriage often begins with shared goals and values. Working together allows you to align your aspirations, values, and dreams, ensuring that you're both on the same page when it comes to building a life together.

Marriage should create a built-in support system. When you work together, you share life's joys and provide each other with emotional, mental, and, in many cases, even financial support during difficult times. Every marriage encounters problems and challenges. Working together enables you to tackle these issues as a team.

You can pool your resources, intelligence, and creativity to find solutions and overcome obstacles. Effective communication is one of the cornerstones of a successful marriage. You build trust, ensure understanding, and maintain a strong emotional connection by working together and communicating openly.

Working together fosters emotional intimacy. As you collaborate on various aspects of your life, you learn to understand and empathize with each other's feelings and needs. In a marriage, responsibilities often need to be divided. Working together ensures a fair and balanced distribution of tasks, such as household chores, childcare, lawn care, and financial management. This can prevent one individual from feeling overwhelmed or unsupported. Working together means making time for each other. Whether it's setting aside time for date nights, shared hobbies, or simply being present in each other's lives, quality time helps strengthen your bond. Marriage can be an opportunity for personal growth.

When you work together, you can learn from each other, adapt to different perspectives, and become better versions of yourselves. Conflict is natural in any relationship, so don't expect it to be any different in a marriage. When you work together to resolve conflicts, you learn to compromise and find common ground.

This resolves immediate issues and helps you avoid repeating the same conflicts in the future.

Marriage is a long-term commitment. By working together, you reinforce your commitment to the relationship, recognizing that the success of the marriage requires ongoing effort, cooperation, and adaptability.

Working together to create a life full of shared experiences and memories strengthens your connection. These shared memories help solidify your bond and provide a sense of togetherness.

If you choose to have children, working together becomes even more essential. It's important in parenting that a stable and loving environment is created for your children to ensure their well-being.

Working together means being invested in each other's happiness and the success of the marriage. It's about collaboration, mutual support, and the shared effort to overcome life's challenges and celebrate its joys. When both spouses actively participate in making the marriage work, they are more likely to build a strong, enduring, and fulfilling relationship.

The foundation of a successful marriage is built on love, trust, and commitment. It's about understanding that the journey you embarked upon together is a partnership, and partnerships require effort from both sides. It's not a competition where one spouse tries to "win" or get their way over the other. Instead, it's about working together to please each other through life's ups and downs.

Just because one person in a relationship may have gotten what they wanted the last time doesn't mean the other individual can expect things to go their way the next time. Marriage is not about "you got what you wanted last time, so this time, I can get what I want." All decisions concerning the direction of the marriage, purchases, etc., should be based on what's best for the marriage and the individuals involved.

It should not be about you got what you want, so now I get what I want or tit for tat. As adults, there should be a level of maturity exemplified. Just because one individual in a relationship may have gotten what they wanted the last time doesn't mean that the other individual can come back and say, well, you got what you wanted last time, so this time I can get what I want.

This is not elementary school, as you talk about being in a relationship that could possibly lead to marriage; you're talking about adults and what it means to be an adult. There should be a certain level of maturity that comes with adulthood, hood, and what's best for the marriage and the individuals involved.

To love your spouse is to tell the truth, even if it's not the most popular response. Marriage isn't about blindly saying yes to every request, as this can lead to resentment and imbalance within the relationship. It's about being open and honest, even when you disagree. It's about expressing your desires and concerns while listening to your spouse.

No two people will ever agree on everything. It's a natural part of being human. Disagreements are inevitable, and they don't necessarily indicate a failing marriage. What's more important is how you handle these disagreements. Instead of just saying yes to avoid conflict, engaging in open and respectful communication is often better.

This involves expressing your own viewpoint and being willing to listen to your spouse's perspective. Trust is the cornerstone of any strong marriage. When you're honest with your spouse, you build trust, and trust is the foundation of emotional security and intimacy. Without trust, a marriage can become shaky and fragile.

Honesty fosters open and effective communication. When you can honestly express your thoughts, feelings, and concerns, you create a safe space for your spouse to do the same. This promotes understanding and connection. Honesty is essential in resolving conflicts. It allows both individuals to express their perspectives and work toward finding mutually acceptable solutions.

Being truthful about your feelings and concerns can lead to constructive discussions.

Emotional intimacy is a key component of a strong marriage. Being honest with your spouse about your emotions, vulnerabilities, and experiences can help you feel more connected and closer to one another.

When you're not honest, it can lead to resentment and frustration. Bottling up your feelings or telling white lies may seem harmless initially, but over time, they can erode the trust and loyalty in your marriage. Honesty demonstrates respect for your spouse. It shows that you value their opinion and are willing to be upfront with them, and it is a way of honoring your spouse's right to know the truth.

A marriage built on a foundation of honesty is more likely to withstand challenges and adversity. When both spouses are truthful with each other, they can face difficulties as a united front.

Honesty makes your actions and words reliable. Your spouse knows they can trust what you say and rely on your promises, which contributes to a sense of safety in the relationship.

Being honest with your spouse can also lead to personal growth and self-awareness. It encourages self-reflection and a deeper understanding of your own emotions and motivations.

Honesty can lead to long-term happiness in your marriage. When you are honest with your spouse, you are more likely to resolve issues, enjoy a solid emotional connection, and experience fulfillment from a healthy, trusting relationship.

It is not just a virtue in marriage; it's an essential ingredient for a strong and enduring relationship. Honesty creates a climate of trust, effective communication, and emotional intimacy. While there may be challenging conversations and moments when honesty feels uncomfortable, the long-term benefits of a truthful and open marriage are well worth it.

Marriage is not about always getting what you want. It's not about constantly making sacrifices or saying yes when you don't mean it. It's about finding a balance, a middle ground where both spouses can feel valued and understood. This means that sometimes you might say yes to your spouse's wishes, and other times you might need to say no.

The key is understanding that decisions are made to support the marriage as a whole. The guiding principle in making decisions should be what is best for the marriage. This approach fosters a sense of unity and shared purpose. It's about being willing to compromise, make sacrifices when necessary, and work together to find mutually satisfying solutions.

Acceptance and compromise are vital components of a successful and enduring marriage. These elements play a crucial role in creating a harmonious and satisfying relationship. you demonstrate unconditional love by accepting your spouse for who they are, flaws, and all. It's the kind of love that is not contingent on your spouse meeting certain conditions or expectations. Reducing judgment in the marriage also comes from acceptance.

When you truly accept your spouse, you are less likely to criticize, nag, or try to change them. This fosters a more positive and supportive atmosphere. When your spouse feels accepted by you, they experience emotional safety. This safety allows them to be themselves without fear of rejection or judgment, encouraging them to be open and honest with you.

Acceptance boosts your spouse's self-worth and self-esteem. Knowing they are loved and valued for who they are can lead to greater confidence and self-assurance. Every individual is unique, and differences between spouses are common. Acceptance allows you to embrace these differences, seeing them as opportunities for growth and learning rather than as sources of conflict.

Compromise is essential for resolving conflicts in a marriage. It involves finding a middle ground or solutions that both individuals can agree on. This is a crucial skill for maintaining harmony and preventing ongoing disputes. In a marriage, there will be times when your needs and desires differ from your spouse's.

Compromise helps balance these competing needs, ensuring that both individuals feel heard and valued. Fairness and equity in marriage are promoted by compromise. It reinforces the idea that both individuals' needs and opinions are important and should be considered. In addition, compromise is an investment in long-term happiness.

It may mean giving up something in the short term, but it often leads to a more content and fulfilling marriage in the long run. The act of compromise strengthens the marriage. It demonstrates a willingness to work together, make sacrifices when needed, and prioritize the relationship's health over individual desires.

It encourages flexibility and adaptability in both individuals. As well as teach you to adjust and accommodate to each other's needs, which can be valuable not only in your marriage but in life as a whole. When a person and their spouse are skilled at compromise, they can often prevent conflicts from escalating. By finding common ground early, you reduce the likelihood of major disagreements.

Acceptance and compromise are two essential building blocks of a thriving marriage. Acceptance creates an atmosphere of love, trust, and emotional security, while compromise fosters conflict resolution and fairness. By embracing these principles, one can build a resilient and fulfilling marriage that stands the test of time.

Marriage, like life itself, has its hills and valleys. There will be good times, and there will be challenging times. A successful marriage can weather these storms, adapt, and grow stronger as a result. It's about having the resilience to navigate through difficulties together. Maturity in marriage means acknowledging that things won't always go as planned, and that's okay.

It means understanding that the love and commitment that brought you together should serve as the guiding light, even in the darkest of moments. When you work together to face life's challenges, you strengthen your marriage and foster a deeper bond and a sense of togetherness.

Recognizing that marriage has its ups and downs is a realistic perspective.

Unrealistic expectations that marriage should always be perfect can lead to disappointment and frustration when difficulties arise, people change over time, and life presents various challenges. These changes can affect the dynamics of a marriage. Understanding these ups and downs allows you to adapt to these changes, manage your expectations, and grow together as a couple.

A marriage that can weather the storms and adapt to the ups and downs will likely be more resilient. Couples can strengthen their bond, learn from their experiences, and develop the skills necessary to overcome future obstacles during challenging times. The hills and valleys of marriage often necessitate improved communication and problem-solving skills.

Couples must learn to express their feelings and concerns during difficult times and work together to find solutions. These skills contribute to a more effective and harmonious relationship. The valleys in a marriage can make the high points even more special.

When you've weathered a challenging period together and emerged stronger, you have a greater appreciation for the good times. This can lead to deeper gratitude and connection.

Understanding the highs and lows of marriage reinforces the commitment to a long-lasting marriage. Recognizing that rough patches are a part of the journey reminds couples of the love and dedication that brought them together in the first place. Experiencing the highs and lows often leads to personal growth and maturity. Couples learn to navigate challenges, compromise, and adapt. These experiences contribute to personal development as well as the growth of the marriage.

The highs and lows create a shared history for the couple. Experiencing and overcoming challenges together builds a stronger connection and a unique bond that is forged through shared experiences. The lows in a marriage can serve as valuable learning experiences. Couples can gain insights into their own behaviors, their spouse's needs, and the dynamics of their marriage. This newfound knowledge can be used to create a more resilient and fulfilling marriage. While "Just Say Yes" may sound like a simple recipe for a happy marriage, the reality is more complex. A successful marriage is built on a foundation of honesty, love, trust, and commitment that thrives on open and honest communication, acceptance, and compromise.

It's about working together to please each other and to support the marriage as a whole. By understanding the highs and lows, hills and valleys, ebb and flow of marriage, and approaching it with maturity, you can build a long-lasting and fulfilling marriage with your spouse.

CHAPTER 10

REMEMBER WHAT'S IMPORTANT

In marriage, it's easy to get caught up in the daily grind, lose sight of what brought you together, and forget the very essence of your union. As time goes by, you change physically and emotionally, life introduces new challenges, and responsibilities begin to pile up. You must remember what's truly important in your marriage and how to nurture it, especially in the toughest of times.

After years of marriage, your focus may be geared more toward the children and their activities instead of your spouse. Focusing and providing for the children is important but not as important as attending to the needs and concerns of your spouse. If the marriage has moved more toward the focus of the children, then when the children grow up and leave home, it causes you and your spouse to end up being roommates or two individuals who no longer share the same interests and desires.

Remember, the two of you met at the altar and pledged I do way before children came into the picture. This is a dangerous place for a married couple to be in because, in most cases, there have been years of inattentive living that have caused for there to be a rift in the marriage, which was once solid. By no means am I saying that the children are not important, but I am saying that one day, the children will grow up, go to college or the military, move out, and be on their own.

At this time, you and your spouse find yourselves at home alone in an empty nest, and in some cases, you feel like strangers due to the inability to keep the closeness and focus on the marriage.

The evolution of marriage is a complex and multifaceted journey that has seen significant changes over time.

While the core principles of love, commitment, and loyalty remain constant, the way marriage is understood, practiced, and legally recognized has evolved over centuries. In ancient societies, marriage was often more of a social and economic contract than a union based on romantic love. It was a means to forge alliances, exchange property or wealth, and secure lineage. Romantic love was not a primary consideration.

Marriage in medieval Europe was still heavily influenced by economic and political considerations. The church played a significant role in regulating and sanctifying marriages. Love often had a limited role in marriage choices. The 18th and 19th centuries brought significant changes in how marriage was perceived.

Romantic love and personal choice began to play a more prominent role in marriage decisions. This shift is often associated with the Romantic movement, which emphasized the importance of individual feelings. The legal aspects of marriage have evolved considerably. Laws regarding who can marry, divorce, and inherit property have seen major changes, particularly in the 20th and 21st centuries.

In addition, Same-sex marriage has gained acceptance and legality in many parts of the world.

The evolution of marriage is closely tied to changing gender roles. Traditional roles of men and women have been challenged, and there is a greater emphasis on equality in modern marriages. Both partners often work outside the home and share responsibilities.

While monogamous marriage remains the dominant form in many societies, the acceptance of polygamy and consensual non-monogamous relationships has grown. These relationships involve multiple partners with full knowledge and consent. In some parts of the world, cohabitation, or living together without formal marriage, has become increasingly common. It's seen as a precursor or alternative to marriage and often carries similar legal rights and responsibilities.

The age at which people marry has risen in many parts of the world. People are focusing on education and careers before tying the knot. This reflects changing priorities and social expectations. Traditional nuclear families are no longer the sole norm. Blended families, single-parent families, and families with same-sex parents have become more common, reflecting greater diversity in family structures.

The rise of the internet and online dating platforms has transformed how people meet and connect. It has expanded the pool of potential partners and allowed individuals to be more selective about their choices. Marriage customs and traditions vary widely across different cultures and regions.

What is considered a typical marriage in one culture may differ significantly from another. Understanding and respecting these differences is crucial in your increasingly globalized world.

In many societies, the stigma attached to divorce has lessened. This shift has allowed individuals to exit unhappy or unhealthy marriages easier, promoting personal well-being and autonomy.

Today, love is often considered a fundamental basis for marriage. The idea of marrying for companionship, emotional support, and shared goals has gained prominence. The evolution of marriage is ongoing and closely intertwined with broader societal changes and shifts in cultural norms.

What remains constant, however, is the significance of the relationship, support, and love that marriage represents in the lives of those who choose to commit to it. As society continues to evolve, so too will the institution of marriage. "Remembering what brought you together" is vital to maintaining a healthy and loving relationship, especially in a marriage.

Over time, it's easy to get caught up in the daily routines and challenges, forgetting the qualities, moments, and feelings that initially attracted you to your spouse. Take time to reminisce about the early days of your relationship. Recall the moments that made you fall in love. This could include the first date, special anniversaries, or unique experiences together.

Open, honest, and empathetic communication in addition to sharing your feelings, thoughts, and desires with your spouse, are crucial. Be an active listener to understand their perspective as well. Healthy communication builds a deeper connection.

In the midst of busy lives, carve out quality time for one another. This doesn't have to be elaborate; even simple, unplugged moments can be precious. Date nights, weekend getaways, or quiet dinners at home are all opportunities to reconnect. Express gratitude and appreciation for your spouse.

Acknowledge their strengths, efforts, and the positive changes you've seen in them. Compliments and thank-you go a long way in making your spouse feel loved and valued. Reconnect with shared interests and hobbies that initially brought you together. Engaging in activities that both enjoy can reignite the sense of camaraderie and closeness.

Surprise your spouse with thoughtful gestures. It could be a love letter, their favorite meal, or a small gift. These surprises show that you're thinking of them and appreciate their presence in your life. Traveling together can be a wonderful way to create new memories and experiences. Exploring new places and trying new things as a couple can add excitement to your marriage.

Physical intimacy is an important part of a marriage. Don't neglect this aspect of your connection. Keep the flame alive by nurturing your marriage and being attentive to your spouse's needs. Discuss and plan for your shared future. What are your dreams and aspirations as a couple?

Working toward common goals can help you stay focused on the bigger picture of your marriage. Don't forget to have fun together. Laughter and playfulness are integral to any successful relationship. Light-hearted moments can strengthen your bond. Sometimes, seeking the guidance of a professional therapist or counselor can be helpful.

They can provide strategies for improving communication, resolving conflicts, and reigniting the emotional connection. Don't neglect your own self-care and personal growth. When both spouses are individually fulfilled and growing, it can positively impact the marriage. Remembering what brought you together and actively working on nurturing these aspects of your marriage is an ongoing process.

It's about showing love, care, and appreciation for your spouse, even as life's challenges evolve. You can keep the love and connection alive by consistently investing in your marriage and staying attuned to each other's needs. In a lasting marriage, adaptation is key. As individuals and circumstances change, the relationship must evolve with them.

Accept your spouses as they are, both physically and emotionally. Love them for who they've become, not who they used to be. This acceptance creates an environment of trust and security in the marriage. During the most challenging times, offer support and understanding. Life's challenges can be overwhelming, but having a spouse who stands by your side can make all the difference.

If children are in the picture, balancing your roles as parents is crucial. While parenthood is a significant responsibility, remember that the foundation of a happy family is a strong and loving marriage. Make time for each other, even amidst the chaos of parenting. Growing as a couple means adapting together.

You may find new interests, discover fresh passions, and set new goals. Embrace these changes and embark on the journey of growth as a unit. Sometimes, the toughest times in a marriage are truly challenging, and seeking professional help or counseling can provide invaluable support. There's no shame in asking for assistance when you need it.

The power of resilience is a critical component of any successful and enduring marriage. Resilience is the ability to bounce back from challenges, adapt to adversity, and maintain a strong, healthy relationship, even in difficult times. Here's why resilience is so important in marriage and how it can help spouses weather the storms together:

Life is full of unexpected challenges, from financial difficulties to health crises and from job loss to the loss of loved ones. Resilience allows a couple to face these challenges together and come through them stronger. Instead of letting these trials tear the marriage apart, resilient couples see them as opportunities to grow together.

Resilience in a marriage means having the ability to navigate conflicts effectively. Rather than letting disagreements escalate into significant issues, resilient couples can address their differences constructively, finding compromises and solutions that strengthen the relationship. This includes the capacity to forgive and let go of past hurts.

In any marriage, there will be times when one or both spouses make mistakes or cause discomfort and even pain. Resilient spouses can forgive and move forward rather than hold onto grudges that erode the marriage. It's also about having shared goals and values to guide the marriage through turbulent times.

Knowing what you want and working towards those goals can provide a sense of purpose and unity. Resilient partners are supportive of one another during difficult times. They offer comfort, encouragement, and empathy, helping each other to cope with stress and challenges. Open and honest communication is crucial to resilience.

Spouses who can talk openly about their feelings, needs, and concerns build trust, the foundation of a resilient marriage. It involves celebrating the positive milestones in your marriage, such as anniversaries and achievements. These celebrations remind you of the strength and love that has carried you through difficult times. As couples see adversity as an opportunity to learn and grow, challenges can be a chance to develop new skills, gain wisdom, and deepen your understanding of each other.

Resilience is about finding the right balance between autonomy and togetherness. Each individual needs to maintain their identity and interests while still nurturing the bond of the marriage. In some cases, the power of resilience includes the willingness to seek professional help or counseling when faced with severe challenges.

A skilled therapist or pastor can provide guidance and tools to help you both navigate difficult situations. Remember to be adaptable. Life is constantly changing, and being open to adapting to new circumstances, roles, and challenges is essential for maintaining a healthy marriage. It also requires taking care of yourself as an individual.

When you're emotionally and mentally strong, you are better equipped to contribute positively to your marriage. Resilience in marriage is about the ability to withstand adversity and come out on the other side stronger. It's the capacity to adapt to change, communicate effectively, and support each other emotionally.

Resilient couples focus on what they can control and work together to overcome challenges, knowing their love and marriage can endure even the most challenging times.

Marriage is a beautiful journey filled with twists and turns. Remembering what's important is the compass that can guide you through the most challenging times. As you and your spouse change physically and emotionally, as children come into the picture and life's challenges test your love, always remind yourselves of the qualities and moments that brought you together.

Embrace change, support one another, and nurture a marriage through it all. Resilience will see you through the storms, and a strong marriage can emerge even stronger on the other side.

So, hold onto what's important, cherish the love you share, and keep the flame of your marriage burning, no matter what life throws your way.

CHAPTER 11

ABSENCE CAN MAKE A DIFFERENCE

The absence of a father or mother can play a significant role in how you see life, relationships, marriage, etc. The inability to build a close, meaningful relationship with a mother or father can shape your viewpoint later in life in how you interact with people in your relationships and of the opposite sex.

My Dad grew up in a single-parent household where my grandmother was the sole provider. Unfortunately, his father was not an active participant in his nurture, maturity, and upkeep. Living in the absence of a parent and, in his case, a father. This caused him to take images of various male figures in his community, a teacher, coach, pastor, etc.

The lack of a resident father caused him to have to "pull together" or "figure out" what a man was from various community figures. It is important to be active in your children's lives so they are not confused about who they are, what is expected of them, and where they are going in life.

Parental absence can have a profound impact on your lives and the way it influences your relationships.

Learning strategies for coping with such absences are beneficial for how you see and enter healthy future relationships. Parents play a fundamental role in shaping your life and perceptions of the world. They are the first individuals you form emotional connections with, and the dynamics of these early relationships can have a long-lasting impact on your emotional and psychological development.

A loving, supportive, and present parent can provide a secure foundation for a child's growth, while the absence of a parent can lead to various challenges. The absence of a father is a significant and complex issue that can have a profound impact on individuals, particularly when it comes to their emotional, psychological, and social development.

This absence can result from various circumstances, such as divorce, separation, abandonment, or the death of a father. Understanding the effects of an absent father is crucial for addressing its challenges and finding ways to cope and thrive. The emotional impact of an absent father can be deeply felt, especially by children.

Children may feel a sense of abandonment, which can lead to emotional distress, feelings of rejection, and a lowered sense of self-worth. These emotional scars can persist into adulthood, affecting self-esteem and self-confidence. The absence of a father, particularly due to death, can trigger profound grief and loss.

Coping with this loss can be an ongoing process that influences emotional well-being. Children may develop difficulties in forming secure attachments and trusting others. This can affect their ability to build healthy relationships, as they might fear being abandoned or rejected. Without the emotional guidance of a father figure, children may struggle with emotional regulation, leading to mood swings, impulsivity, and difficulty coping with stress and anxiety.

The absence of a father can affect a child's academic performance and motivation. They may struggle with school, leading to lower grades and limited educational opportunities. A father's absence can affect the development of a child's sense of identity, particularly their understanding of masculinity and their place in society.

It can impact how individuals perceive and interact with others, particularly in romantic relationships and interactions with the opposite sex. Individuals who grew up without a father might struggle to form intimate relationships, as they may fear abandonment or rejection. The emotional issues stemming from a father's absence can carry over into adult relationships, leading to communication difficulties, trust issues, and conflicts.

A father's absence can influence how individuals perceive masculinity and men in general, potentially leading to skewed or negative views. Therapists and counselors can provide support in processing the emotional impact and developing coping strategies. Surrounding oneself with friends and family who provide emotional support and understanding is crucial.

Taking time to reflect on the impact of a father's absence on one's life can be a valuable step in understanding and addressing issues. Consciously working on building healthy relationships and seeking role models or mentors can counter the negative effects of a father's absence. The absence of a mother is another complex and impact issue that can significantly affect individuals. This absence can result from various circumstances, such as divorce, separation, or the death of a mother. Understanding the effects of an absent mother is crucial for addressing its challenges and finding ways to cope and thrive. The emotional impact of an absent mother can be profound, particularly for children. It can manifest in several ways.

This loss, especially due to death, can trigger intense grief and feelings of profound loss. Coping with this loss can be an ongoing emotional struggle. Children may experience emotional instability, given the significant emotional support that mothers typically provide. This can lead to mood swings, difficulty coping with stress, and anxiety.

An absent mother can result in attachment issues, making it challenging for children to form secure emotional bonds with others. This can affect their ability to build healthy relationships later in life. It can also impact a child's sense of identity, including their understanding of femininity and their place in society.

The absence of a mother means that children do not have a maternal role model to learn from, potentially impacting their ability to be nurturing parents themselves. Those who have grown up without a mother may need to actively seek out resources and support to learn effective parenting skills.

Children who lack a mother's influence might have a less clear understanding of femininity and women's roles in society. This can lead to questions about the roles and responsibilities of caregivers, particularly within a family structure. Coping with the absence of a mother is crucial for personal growth and well-being.

Therapists and counselors can provide support in processing the emotional impact and developing coping strategies. Surrounding oneself with friends and family who offer emotional support and understanding is vital. Reflecting on the impact of a mother's absence on one's life can be a valuable step in understanding and addressing issues.

Actively working on building healthy relationships and seeking role models or mentors can help individuals counter the negative effects of a mother's absence. A mother's absence can profoundly impact individuals, shaping their emotional, psychological, and social development. Recognizing these effects, seeking support, and actively working to address the challenges of a mother's absence can help individuals build healthy, fulfilling lives and relationships despite the absence of a mother's influence.

It's a journey of self-discovery, healing, and personal growth that many have successfully undertaken. Coping with parental absence, whether it's the absence of a father, mother, or both, is a challenging and deeply personal journey. The emotional and psychological impact of such absence can be profound.

Still, there are strategies and steps that individuals can take to cope with these challenges and move forward in a healthy and fulfilling way. Therapists, counselors, and support groups can provide valuable assistance in dealing with the emotional and psychological challenges associated with parental absence.

A trained professional can help one explore their feelings, develop coping strategies, and provide a safe space to express your emotions. Surround yourself with friends, family, and a support network who can offer emotional support and understanding. Sharing your experiences with those you trust can be therapeutic and help alleviate feelings of isolation.

Take time to reflect on how parental absence has influenced your life. Self-awareness is a crucial step in understanding and addressing any resulting issues. Journaling, meditation, and self-reflection can be helpful tools in this process. Consciously work on building healthy relationships with friends and loved ones.

Seek out role models or mentors who can provide guidance and support in areas where one may have been impacted by parental absence. Reconnecting with an absent parent can be a healing experience for some individuals. It provides an opportunity to ask questions, seek closure, and potentially rebuild a relationship.

However, this option should be carefully considered, as the parents you seek may not always welcome it. If re-connection with an absent parent is not possible or welcomed, look for healthy role models in your life. This might include mentors, family friends, teachers, or other supportive individuals who can provide guidance and support.

If you have experienced parental absence, be aware of the potential impact on your own parenting skills. Strive to break negative cycles by seeking guidance and education on effective parenting techniques. Understanding the challenges can help you become a more nurturing and supportive parent.

Develop emotional resilience and coping skills to manage the emotional challenges associated with parental absence. Techniques like mindfulness, stress management, and self-compassion can be valuable in maintaining emotional well-being. View the process of coping with parental absence as an opportunity for personal growth and healing.

Overcoming these challenges can make you stronger and more resilient, allowing you to lead a fulfilling life despite the absence of a parent. In some cases, finding a path to forgiveness and acceptance can be a crucial step in the healing process. This may involve forgiving the absent parent or accepting the circumstances surrounding their absence.

For cases where parental absence has resulted in severe emotional trauma, addiction, or other complex issues, it's essential to consult with professionals who specialize in those areas, such as addiction counselors, psychologists, or social workers. Coping with parental absence is a journey that requires time, patience, and self-compassion.

It's important to remember that everyone's experience is unique, and there is no one-size-fits-all solution. Seeking help and support and actively working on personal growth and healing can lead to a more fulfilling and emotionally balanced life despite the challenges of parental absence.

Reconnecting with an absent parent or developing new relationships is another important aspect of coping with parental absence.

While this might not always be possible or the best choice, it's often worth exploring. Reconnecting with an absent parent can be a healing experience for some individuals. It provides an opportunity to ask questions, seek closure, and potentially rebuild a relationship. However, as previously expressed, if re-connection is not possible or welcomed, seeking healthy role models to fill the void is crucial. This might include mentors, family, friends, or other supportive individuals.

Forming strong, nurturing relationships with friends and loved ones can help compensate for the absence of a parent and provide the emotional support needed for personal growth. The absence of a father or mother can have a profound and lasting impact on your life, particularly in how you approach relationships, marriage, and interactions with others.

It's essential to acknowledge these effects, seek support when necessary, and take proactive steps to overcome the challenges posed by parental absence. Individuals can build healthy, fulfilling lives and relationships, even without a parent's influence. As the parent of a child, please understand how important it is to be visible, present, and active in your child's life.

No parent is perfect, but it is vitally important to be present and positive. Spending quality time with your child builds a lasting bond that can be shared for years. In addition, you positively affect the next generation and their outlook on yourselves, their peers, and their relationships.

CHAPTER 12

PRAYERFUL AND CAREFUL

As you have gone through the various stages of friendship to marriage and beyond, it's important that you are prayerful and careful when evaluating an individual for a long-term relationship. Being open and honest from the very beginning and expressing these feelings is a crucial component of making your expectations, needs, and goals known.

To withhold your true feelings about issues, topics, goals, and expectations is a set-up for relationship failure. you must not allow yourself to settle for less than God's best for you by holding back on your goals, expectations, desires, and dreams. So often, you settle for less when it comes to relationship choices, and because of your settling, you end up miserable.

Ensure that God is first in your daily lives and relationships. As you take your focus off of people and things and put your focus on God, He will provide for your every need. God gives you time to work on your relationship with Him and with yourself. Sometimes, God wants you to deal with your own issues, concerns, and character flaws before you add another person into the equation.

Use this time as a single person to self-correct and improve yourself. It's important to be the best version of oneself that one can be. If this means pursuing a better job, refraining from cursing, strengthening your relationship with God, making wise investments, or even letting go of people in your life who are weighing you down, then now is the time.

This life that God has given you is too short to live in misery. you need to manage your mental well-being, reduce stress and do things that make you happy and give God glory. If you live your life and are miserable in your relationship and daily activities, then it's time to evaluate your situation and make positive changes.

To choose an appropriate partner, one must first be grounded and have a proper understanding of who they are and what they desire in a relationship. Knowing oneself is vital when deciding to enter into a relationship because if one doesn't know what one wants and doesn't want, like, and dislike, then there is no way another person can learn how to please a person or abide by their wishes.

Be mindful that every person who enters into your life does not necessarily deserve to have access to your life. you live in a day and an age where everyone does not deserve to have access to us. Be very picky when it comes to choosing a partner. Take your time, ask questions, and evaluate wisely.

Asking questions of a potential partner gives you insight into this person's background, lifestyle, likes, dislikes, and future goals. It provides one input into whether this person can possibly be a compatible match for you. Pay close attention to any red flags that may arise as a result of answers to your questions that you feel should have been answered differently according to your goals.

Always remember you cannot change people. You can only change yourself. When it comes to people, sometimes what you see is what you get. This is why it's vitally important for you to know what you can and cannot deal with. Because people don't change, you cannot enforce your standards, likes, and lifestyle on them and expect them to thrive in an environment that is not conducive to them.

Simply put, choosing the wrong person as a mate can cause you to fail, both in the relationship and in life. However, choosing the right person can cause you to succeed, soar beyond measure, and reach heights you never thought you could. That's why it's imperative and vital to take your time to evaluate individuals you are considering as a mate.

Don't rush; be efficient, effective, and thorough, and don't allow red flags to go unnoticed and unaddressed. If something is said that you have questions about, ask, "What do you mean by what you said?" This will allow you to have a clear understanding of where this individual's mind is and their mentality about different situations and scenarios.

A wrong choice today can cause you to be miserable for the rest of your life.

YOU CAN DO BAD ALL BY YOURSELF; you don't need another person to come into your life to cause you to do worse than what you are already doing. The person you choose to be your mate should be somebody who can bring completeness to you, accommodate you, assist in making you a better version of yourself, and elevate your current situation.

REMEMBER, be prayerful and careful about selecting a mate, for they should be able to help you reach your goals and dreams, not be the reason for your demise.

ABOUT THE AUTHOR

Dr. John L. Jacobs, III is the son of educators and is a graduate of Talladega College with a BA in Chemistry, Howard University with a Master of Divinity, and an earned Doctor of Ministry from Columbia Theological Seminary. He has worked with the inmate population, homeless community, sick-and-shut-in, at-risk youth, state government, and federal government, served as a Hospice Chaplain, and has been a pastor for more than 20 years. He and his wife, Pamela, are the parents of four children.